THE SILENCE OF THE HORIZONS

Published by Schaffner Press

First English Translation Copyright Schaffner Press, © 2025

Translated by Marjolijn de Jager

Original French language edition titled

"Le silence des horizons" by Mbarek Ould Beyrouk.

Copyright © 2021, Éditions Elyzad, all rights reserved.

Cover and interior book design by Evan Johnston.

Library of Congress Control Number: 2024947048

ISBN: 978-1-63964-068-3

EPUB: 978-1-63964-069-0

EPDF; 978-1-63964-070-6

Manufactured in the United States of America.

# THE
# SILENCE
## OF THE
# HORIZONS

## BEYROUK

TRANSLATED BY
MARJOLIJN DE JAGER

SCHAFFNER PRESS
TUCSON, ARIZONA

TOMORROW NEEDS TO come back, and the colors of the day, and people's smiles, and the sun on girls' cheeks. I don't want to look around me anymore. I want to scan the brilliance of the stars, to read in them the joys that are awaiting me. They have to exist, the hours that caress you, the moments when you feel the evening poems rise inside you. I try to interpret the murmurs of the silence, because everything is silent now, today's turbulence has been smothered, there's only an immense space in me, only the two of us, me and nothingness, or rather me and the whole, I can shout and no one will hear me, I can insult the entire universe, I can take off my clothes and run around freely, I can spout all the drivel in the world, I can even ruminate if I want, everything is possible here, except for other people. Now, beneath this silent blue sky I want to write new words that can bring me absolution. I suppress the looming screams and the cruel images that want to rob me of my life, that are trying to ooze into me, no, I want to quell everything and call for new lights. I want the void inside me so it will wring the neck of truth, yes, what's howling inside me must be extinguished and the sirens of the past must resume.

Perhaps it is Fati who will save me, just seeing her eyes, just holding my loveliest moments with her in my mind, killing off all the rest. She used words that belong to her breasts, yes, soaring words, fluid words, full of life.

*I've seen the fully naked arm*
*And the pulsing throat*
*And the radiant face*
*And the singing eyes*

I see her again humming ancient songs. Whose words were they? Her slender hands would tap her legs and she'd raise her head to the heavens as if to escape from the hour's incessant calls. At moments like that I loved her even more intensely. Yes, maybe she didn't really let me go... Maybe it's merely jealousy, there are words I can say and I'll say them: 'I'm nothing but a poor blind lover who has no idea at all where to go, I want you to show me the way and I will follow it, never again any word or gesture that wouldn't please you, tell me, show me the path that leads to you and I will take it, even if I wear away the soles of my feet, see the water inside me dry up...,' beautiful unguarded things like that, just foliage, no bark, and maybe she'll come back to me.

Yes, this evening I must dwell on the lovely images, the happy memories, dismiss the torments stalking me, erase today, it doesn't exist today, yesterday is all there is and perhaps yesterday is tomorrow.

I have to keep telling myself incessantly: 'That madness doesn't exist, that insane rage, those eyes from which the light is gone, that moment of calamity, it wasn't me, I couldn't have done that, it was a ghastly nightmare, and I woke up here, alone, in the midst of this vastness.'

It must be wiped out, I have to accomplish that much, and I also have to keep repeating: 'nobody saw anything, so nothing happened', I really have to if I want to survive, and besides what is one hour of madness in someone's life, one instant of blindness, why should those few minutes destroy a life, no, I shouldn't let the insanity of one moment take over my existence, I must forget those images and call on other ones, close my eyes and recall the moments of bliss.

How many of them are there?

I no longer know, there is the sea of course, and there is always she.

Fati again, the hours we spent on the beach, a little restaurant, small tents, and our hands furtively squeezing each other's under a table. That afternoon the sea had donned her blueish dress glittering with golden threads, the waves were in a rush to kiss the sand and then go back, leaving white bubbles to slowly evaporate—the sea's saliva, they said—and stay on your lips, children noisily running after them, we weren't talking or hardly, we'd already said it all, I believed we had traced the furrows that our lives would create. That's what it is, I want to live in the time that's past. Raya must not be anymore, she never existed, like that cursed father, like the coolness of the night that permeates me now, I am somewhere else, the pincers of remorse cannot reach me anymore. I must continue on my path, go far away, join Sidi and his friends, run after new worlds and thereby dispel it all.

I resume my route, headlights opening the night's dark doors, the entire world is silent, the silence deafens me, it beckons me to pull myself toward the torments, I obstinately refuse to be drowned in the flood of bad memories, I sing, too, forgotten words come back to my lips, the melodies of my childhood.

*The moon is smiling tonight*
*We should go strolling*

*Near the tents of oblivion*
*To encounter the Beloved*

I should not have left my native village, I should have stayed there and not fallen prey to the gaping mouths that swallow up people's minds and hearts anywhere that there's progress now, I should've chosen a different life. What would my life be if I had stayed, I wouldn't have suffered my mother's oppression nor that of her husband, my father's image might not have been so momentous, I wouldn't have done any formal studies, I wouldn't have taken on this century's anxieties, I would have never asked myself any questions, I wouldn't have known either Fati or Raya, I would have led a different life where I might not have suffered this burning mind, this shame of being me, there are thousands out there everywhere who live life without ever questioning themselves, without a love lost, without any madness inside their head. Perhaps I should go back to my childhood, dig deep down searching for memories in which I can disappear, yes, but to start with all I see are only blurred images, it's like a fog, then suddenly I see people dancing, laughing, sometimes yelling, Karima, our neighbor who liked me a lot, a man kissing her on the mouth, slender fingers brushing my cheek, I was sitting on a large cushion, a packet of cookies in my hand, looking around, and I was happy. And then there were curses, great turmoil, a man who lifted me up from inside the crowd throwing insults around and, once outside, my grandmother who was waiting for us and hugged me tightly as she wept; I found out later that Karima was a bad girl who had taken me to an evening with 'degenerates'. From that moment on my mother prevented her from coming anywhere near me.

Another face comes back to me, Zeina, a friend of my grandmother's, younger than she, with bright eyes and a big smile, I was in love with her and, suddenly shy when she'd come to the house, my pranks would stop, I would become a docile obedient child and my grandmother would order me around with her finger as she winked at her, the two of them laughing while I just wanted to wet my pants.

Yes, I must find refuge elsewhere, not allow any room for remorse to surface. Sidi is waiting for me with his friends.

Nothing moves around me, the Sahara is falling asleep, at times the ghosts of a cabin, a tent, a dilapidated hovel emerge from the darkness then fade away, a bird, I don't know what kind, skims by my windshield on the right; that should be a good sign I tell myself, and then suddenly in the distance lights that remind me of time, Akjoujt.

Akjoujt has hung on too long to move anymore, it became lifeless a long time ago, worn out by the waves of predators that have been sucking it dry for a century, first a colonial fort, then a mine followed by another mine, they kept going at the earth-covered body until there was no sap left to secrete and its heart gave out. It faded away more than once, then, under the heavily breathing appetites of gigantic corporations, its fires were reluctantly relit, but the crude rapists' deep shadows were permanently imprinted on its flaking walls. I won't stop here, these common shops, these filthy heartless restaurants, these life-abandoned shacks can't hold me here, all that remain are souls leaving for the mine, for the north, for the south, everyone is merely passing through, it's true that I know life continues over there, farther away, in the isolated area where people still cling to a lost town, in the surrounding desert where they live as if the world was frozen long ago, and in the eyes of those who fled as well and who, from afar, sketch in words the idyllic memory of a vanished Akjoujt. But nostalgia is no longer even felt on these rambling avenues, which refuse to stop in front of the worm-eaten doors of yesteryear's town. The city offers only the damaged surface of a lost land.

How did Raya come into my world? I didn't invite her. How did she dare seek to impose herself on me?

I got back on the road with a sandstorm sweeping through my head and in my eyes, I was thinking about nothing, all I felt was an enormous void inside, my conscience was obscured, a dense fog enveloped my mind, although I was lucid because I saw the road clearly and avoided freely roaming animals. I knew where Sidi and his friends would be camping that night, at the Labiadh wadi, the white wadi, an immense river of sand embraced by bluish mountains.

A few dispersed huts, a few clay houses, one or two distant villas, this is Yaghref, a village that has lost its calling, agriculture, a spillway where the mountain waters converged and where they cultivated barley, millet, watermelons, but the waters no longer reach here, the desert has licked half of the arable areas clean, the new towns have devoured the youth of the village, and those who stay now prefer to run behind animals or run small businesses on the road. I stop at one of them and call the saleswoman who's sitting on a mat, absorbed by her cell phone. 'I would like some cigarettes and a bottle of water,' she doesn't get up, 'Just come and help yourself,' she tells me with a scornful look. I go down, enter her shop, take my items and go back to pay her. This time she smiles at me. 'The drivers who pass by have an attitude sometimes, so we like to cut them down to size,' she now apologizes cheerfully. She has a handsome face, a smile that lights up her smooth cheeks, and eyes that invite conversation, but I don't say a word, I don't want to leave any sign of my presence nor do I want to be remembered.

Suddenly the Labiadh wadi opens its arms to me. The rolling white ground, streaked with vague folds, occupies the entire view, and in the distance, stifled up to the gorge by indomitable dunes, mountains impassively witness the victory of sand and winds. The tires of the car are struggling on this terrain that's ready to swallow them whole, I activate the coupling and clutch the steering wheel.

How did I get here? I was blind, and in my confusion one name came to me. Sidi! I had gone with him to the Banc d'Arguin National Park where he was taking some tourists. A nice group, three couples, two single people, three children. They come almost every year. I became friends with the children. I promised them a story, they were thrilled. Sidi wanted me to follow them to Adrar, I said yes, just like that, without really thinking that I would. A premonition?

Ever since I've known him Sidi has always been a refuge. I used to run to him to keep the ghosts away and silence the alarming questions for a moment. He'd talk to me about his profession, his encounters, his clients who often became his friends. 'They come here to get away, I take them to the great desert, I have them visit the ancient *ksours*—the fortified villages, the old cities, the abandoned oases. They really love it. They break away from their world, their routines, their daily rut, from the grand hotels as well, and often they find themselves again, they discover who they are.'

It's to get away that I sometimes come to be with Sidi, when I'm with him I can stop my questions, I've even toyed with the idea of becoming a guide someday, 'you don't need to study for that,' he explained, 'sites whose history you have to know, a desert that tells its own story, some anecdotes here and there, simple fare you should know how to prepare, polite nicely turned expressions, keeping the atmosphere cheerful, that's all there's to it. Knowing some small local theater groups and having them perform occasionally, knowing how to pitch a tent, and how to walk of course. It doesn't bring in a lot of money but it's fun, you meet plenty of people and discover new things every day, you just have to like it.' But my father was the best guide the country ever had. A good reason to steer clear from this job!

I reached the camp at daybreak, they were finishing their breakfast, getting ready to head off, they were very pleased to see me but they had to leave, the children clung to me but I couldn't go with them. Neither Sidi nor his friends had anything to say, just welcoming smiles, so there was nothing written on my face it would seem, or perhaps they were still half asleep or maybe because of the turban that was hiding part of my head. I really spoke to no one, I just said: 'Excuse me but I'm dead tired,' and dove into a tent, quickly opened a package of sleeping pills that I always have with me and took one. I buried myself under a blanket. I felt feverish, my whole body was shaking, shadows were pursuing me, a deep groan. I sank into a restless sleep.

I woke up late, came out of the tent and looked around. Nature seems to have abandoned me, keeps silent and gives me a nasty look. Nothing speaks to me any longer. Not the setting sun although it appears to be smiling, nor the dunes that shimmer beneath the sleepy rays, nor the sky already bedecked with evening colors, nor the sterile clouds wandering around, dazed and indecisive. Nothing speaks to me. The turmoil is inside me and the entire universe is mute.

I'm turned toward the sunset and feel my torments coming back, throughout my trip I tried to beat them down, affronted them, chased them, I called upon the spirits, both the good and the evil ones, to overpower them, I closed my eyes to ignore them. Now they're clouding my brain, constricting my innards, suffocating me. War-weary, I finally let them ramble around the muddy waters that provide shelter for my thoughts. I am like a voiceless spectator watching himself pass by, dressed in the rags of his fears and fruitlessly trying to give himself a name. No, they aren't there any longer, the images attempting a rescue, they aren't there any longer those voices of yesterday, my past refuses to come back, the beautiful moments stay silent, there's only me facing my hideous self and the cries that want to escape from a strangled throat.

Still I keep repeating it: it's absurd to moan over elusive ghosts, over emanations that strut about naked in the middle of wastelands. They shouldn't belong to me anymore, these phantoms that roam around inside me, still suffocating me, but they will quickly vanish, they are anxious because they're dying, but it's no longer a matter of time, they will be extinguished tomorrow when I will tell all.

Tomorrow for sure, I will speak, I will return to the city and I will say: 'It's me', I will be sure to say: 'It's me', but now I simply want to listen to myself, let my inner anxieties speak, for once the madness that has always kept quiet should be expressed.

Why did I so easily succumb to the interrogations, the dread, the anguish, the disavowals, the rages, the shame? Why did I let myself be imprisoned by words that they created? How do they concern me, the father I never knew, the mother simultaneously so frail and so strong, the 'holy man' as they say, whose holiness I simply cannot understand?

I don't think I'm a monster, no, that would have been a fine excuse, I don't think I've been marked by destiny, which would have been an excuse as well, I don't think I've lost my mind, that would have been too easy a refuge, when all is said and done I am just a lost soul, survivor of a forgotten vessel, whose ultimate incentives crumbled under the weight of a shipwreck that isn't his.

But is it really I who am the victim today? No, that's an absurd thought: the victim is still there, eyes fixed on the horror, forever, sacrificed on the altar of darkness that is beyond her, too.

I look at my hands, they aren't shaking, although they are quite weak, but they're not shaking, they've written a fatal grin on a candid smile and they aren't shaking. Do they belong to me, these hands whose grooves, bulges, cracks I notice, and that are staying calm, impervious to their own crimes? And this head buzzing not with genuine regrets but with nagging memories? And this gut, still throttled by old agonies, forgetting the felonies of yesterday?

It was only yesterday but it was another life.

Yes, tomorrow, I will go there and I will tell it all.

My mother's cry still resonates within me: 'Is that you, my son? Is that you, my son?' I shut off the cell phone, then broke it into a thousand pieces, threw away the remnants in the middle of the desert, and I ran to create a distance between myself and that voice that came from so far away, I didn't want to hear that anymore either, I fled so that I wouldn't hear anything anymore.

Mama never told me anything. She'd drown my questions with her smiles, her caresses, her gifts, with her anger, and in the end with her tears, she always refused to look back with me; I know she had sworn to forget everything, expunge everything, she did it so she could live, for her husband and for me as well. I don't hold it against her, she believed that I could grow up in the silence. She hates noises and straightforward explanations, too. She was especially afraid of hearing me speak about my father, she would tremble at the thought that I might know. Her life is nothing but an agonizing wait, turned entirely toward the erasure of what has been. But how could she think she could obliterate everything while I was its daily presence?

I know, Mama rejected me at first, she didn't want me living beside her, she entrusted me to her mother who adored me but then she died and Mama really did have to take me back. I was a frail and embarrassing presence because I was the unwanted one, a reminder of the outcast, the pariah, the tainted. But little by little she learned to love me, especially when she found out that she could have no other children.

Ahmed, my mother's husband, never rejected me. Anyway, he never rejected anything, he accepted the whole wide world and smiled at everything. Truth be told, nothing matters to him, the universe could go under and he probably wouldn't know about it until the last moment, he'd listen to the news of the cataclysm with just one ear, and then only if he were forced to. He abides by everything, he understands everything, he never judges anything or anyone, he merely takes note and shakes his head, you feel no anxiety in him, his features betray neither joy nor anger, his animals are his one passion, or Mama, that's true, he really loves Mama, obeys her in everything, he placed his fortune and his relations in her hands while he lives in a tent in the Amessaga or Inchiri regions and runs after his camels. In effect, he's running toward something indefinable, something he doesn't know, toward an impossible blissfulness. But when my grandmother died and Mama had to take me back, he clearly felt that I was in need of attention. It was he who told me stories at night and pampered me, he who bought me toys, took me to parks and to the beach.

Was he a true father to me? No, I believe that he was nothing to anyone except to my mother, he just plays the role that is assigned to him, father, son, friend, cousin, he plays it fast, bored with the obligations that other people, that life, impose on him and afterward he tries to forget, to erase everything, fill his lungs with fresh air and empty his mind. I never learned to love him, yet I never knew how to hate him.

My friends? Night-time drives, moments spent, words flying off, I don't see many faces, many names. First there's Sidi who knows how to look kindly upon things, how to laugh heartily, have fun without going too far, and then he doesn't pay attention to any flaws. Still, we don't have the same background. He comes from a family of poor oasis peasants, he has had very little education, two years of secondary school, he was a driver of transport cars, then gradually learned a few words of French and English by escorting tourists, and soon he became a guide, made lots of friendships, which was easy for him, he's always made friends easily.

Then there are Mahmoud, Bâ, Kader, Moktar, and a few others. Come to think about it, I have quite a number of friends. Nevertheless, I've never felt that bonding, that fusion of sentiments upon which true friendship is based, so they say.

My loves? Fati? How much effort did I have to make not to call her, not to pass by her house, not to utter her name. She had told me no, that's all, she'd looked me straight in the eyes and said 'no' in a tone that held no emotion. I didn't know what that meant, that 'no', I was too stunned to answer and then she left, I no longer had the legs to catch up with her, and I had nothing but hollow words left to respond, to cry out. I felt it as an injustice and I began to speak ill of her, everywhere, 'she's a bad girl', I would say to everyone but did people actually believe me? They looked at me strangely, sometimes even contemptuously, they never answered me, they were speechless. As if I hadn't spoken, 'Fati is a bad girl and I left her because she's a bad girl,' they were like stone. Did they already know that it was she who had rejected me? I didn't want to look like a loser and kept trying to find a pair of eyes that believed me, to find a nod of solidarity somewhere. Nothing. You would've thought she'd bewitched everyone and that nobody wanted to hear from me, so in the end I stopped bad-mouthing her, I kept my pain to myself, that's all. Yes, I know, it's to her that hands reach out, it's for her that beggars smile in the streets, it's always her that children greet... and yet...

And yet, all the arguments she'd presented to the others were simply lies: 'Too spoiled., too dependent, rich man's son.' Maybe, maybe! Let's agree on that. But that's something she should have known from the very first moment on, so these were false pretexts, but I, I know why she left me: it's because of my name, no matter what she says, it's because of my name. Yes, she can shout from every rooftop that she's different, that she wants to change our world, that she's progressive, she may well be photographed next to her father, behind enormous flags, clenching her fist, railing against governments, she may well write pretty poems in which she embraces the entire earth, she remains what basically they all are here, creatures controlled by traditions, by the Cheikh, and all those who, salivating, continue to follow fools for centuries, all over the world.

Ah, still I'd been carefully forewarned, 'she's too old for you and besides she's too free, too educated, too beautiful', yes, she's two years older than I and I know that around here that shouldn't happen. But she cast a spell over me, Fati literally enraptured me, I ran after her for two months so she would finally become aware of my existence, of my eyes that would look for her everywhere, of my heart that would pound when she turned around. I marched for causes that meant nothing to me, a man who had burned a sacred book (he should have just been treated as a jerk because there will always be sacred books), doctors on strike (they should just treat the rich and keep quiet, the poor will go to the marabous), rigged elections (yes, but the opposition candidate is even more corrupt than the one in power), I would discuss subjects that were hardly of any concern to me, and I'd raise my voice to be heard by her. I finally dared to invite her to dinner, by the shore, I hired a whole staff, I pitched two well-equipped tents, armchairs, gold-colored cushions, new carpeting, huge candles as lighting, griots to provide music, excellent cooks, it all cost me a fortune, my mother grumbled but no matter, I wanted to impress Fati and that was worth any sacrifice. Was I successful? Sure, she fell into my arms, but I always felt she was distant, preoccupied with the subjects that scarcely mattered to me, chasing after ambitions that aren't mine, I walked next to her in demonstrations, I was her slave, I eagerly sought to please her, and in the end it seemed that she got tired, she would claim to have a thousand appointments, a thousand meetings, she no longer answered my phone calls. So I went to her front door, I demanded to see her and she came out, then said: 'You didn't get it? It's over between us, over,' I couldn't get a word out, only a soundless, unsteady 'why'. Why? Because of my name, of course, she may have presented a thousand excuses, I know it's because of my name, of the father I've never known and who steals everything from me, even this little window of happiness.

Did I have other loves? Faces and bodies go by. Khadija for a moment, a few weeks. Too good for me, too well educated, too beautiful, too intelligent, too possessive. I no longer belong to myself so I couldn't surrender myself to her. There've been moments that I regretted that. In her arms I might have been able to expunge everything... or suffocate. I've never trusted anyone. I have always been afraid of women because they can guess, because they read flaws, and because they know how to possess. After Khadija I made a game out of conquering and then dropping them, that's what I said, it's what I made my friends believe, but no, the truth is that I would run off as soon as I felt the slightest apathy in them, perceived the first frowns, I was afraid of being defeated again, of reading rejection in their eyes, each time hovering on a word, a gesture, a grimace, I expected to see my father's name reemerge. Khadija almost tamed me, she would caress my faults, give me reasons to be me, she was familiar with my father's past and tried, sometimes awkwardly, to free me of it, but actually I didn't want to forsake my secret sorrows, my resumed complexes, my inner anxieties, and I no longer wanted to give myself, no, I wouldn't assent to giving myself.

This wish to remain oneself and unique, this refusal to be tamed, are they not a reminder of the father I never knew but who too often is with me?

Today I should free myself of the gloom as well as of all that glitters. I have created an enormous rift between me, the others, and life, I have taken the step that relieves me of fragile feelings. I can no longer be anything other than what I am—a man with dirty hands. I have bought their hatred dearly, madly, and this act of lunacy ought to liberate me from the weight of their glares, I should feel nothing anymore because I now live inside a black bubble that separates me from everyone else.

Shadows are beginning to inhabit the land, taking revenge on the day's whiteness as they fling black burnouses over nature and people, sterile clouds stifle the stars, night already rules the universe, dunes have turned into dusky mountains without crests or rims, shrubs into motionless monsters ready to swallow any living presence, crickets croon the heartaches of the night, and the distant bellowing of exhausted camels delineate the anxieties to come.

I'm pleased with this state of things for I know what night reveals: a world without artifice, because I also know that ugliness is the true color of time.

Perhaps the night will protect me when my friends come back. They won't see my drawn face or my distorted features, nor the extreme fatigue that still lives in my eyes. Sidi leaves very few lights on at night, he says they attract insects. But he does allow wood fires.

But maybe my face, my body won't show anything. Maybe the despondency is only within me. I passed in front of Minou, the camel driver, and even said 'Salaam' and he responded to my greeting, he didn't seem at all unsettled when he saw me. So? I slept all day, after all. I should look refreshed, even if I drove all night. I would like to see myself in a mirror but in Sidi's kingdom there's no mirror except in the clients' tents. In any event, I do know that my face doesn't show any nail marks. Her fingers merely grabbed my wrists in a paltry effort to free herself, her mouth opening in a slobbering gurgle.

A slight tremble runs through my body, head spinning a little, stomach going through convulsions, I get up to vomit. I close my eyes and empty my conscience to let the storm pass. That's it, I have to wipe the slate clean completely, forget everything, crush the images that anxiety sends back to me. Tomorrow I will tell all.

I see Raya, and her eyes that lit up when we met for the first time, yes, she kissed me with her eyes and her body moving, calling me again, she was already prepared to go all the way, perhaps she'd put on too much make-up, yes, but she was beautiful. Why did she fall for me so quickly? Was destiny grinning? It was Isma who introduced her to me, just a few words: 'My friend Raya'. We talked a little. Downright  fawning already. Why didn't she tell me from the start that she was the Cheikh's daughter? I would have certainly run from her and nothing would have happened. Just a tiny word and the tragedy wouldn't have occurred. There's an uncertain thread, a buried invisible secret, that may explain the dramatic implications. I who have never believed in anything, I now believe in destinies inscribed once and for all on the tablets of forever. 'It is written', my mother liked to say. Why not?

I remember our conversation well. Isma had left us alone, I didn't know what to say at first for the girl really didn't do anything for me, yet she'd approached me, touching my hips, I even felt her quiver a little.

'It seems you own a very nice car and that you used to see that stuck-up Fati.'

'I don't see the connection.'

'It's just that Fati is boring and with a car like that we could really have fun.'

'Why are you laying into Fati, do you know each other?'

'Oh no, not really, she's older than I am, an old maid already, and I think you're too good for her, luckily you've broken up with her, they say.'

'They say... '

'That's all there is around here, the "they say".'

'But Fati is a fine girl in every respect and I don't like it when people say bad things about her.'

'Oh my! Such generosity of heart, "in every respect", and what about me, am I not good "in every respect"?'

'I wouldn't know.'

'It just depends on you.'

'You sure speak your mind, don't you?'

'Ah yes, I say what I feel, I express myself, I don't dabble in "politics" like your Fati.'

'Anything else?'

'Sure, let's talk about other things, how about you take me out for some fresh air?'

'Impossible right now, I'm waiting for some friends.'

'You know, all those men you see are simply waiting for a sign from me to come running.'

'I don't doubt it, but honestly, I have an appointment, I assure you.'

'So we'll see each other some other time, you'll call me, here is my number.'

'Alright, we'll be sure to see each other again.'

Did I leave any traces on the beach? I don't think so. The wind will obliterate my steps. It blows everything away. Does my body show any sign of my crime? I check myself all over, no, nothing. Surprisingly, destiny's markings didn't put an indelible seal on me, though they should have!

Other cracks are still inside me, immense fissures, never filled, 'assassin's son', 'heathen's son', I found that written on my school desk, then on my notebook, 'he stinks' one student even said one time; I showed it to Mama and told her all about the constant insults, and then sobbed: 'They don't want to play with me anymore at recreation time, they say that I smell like hell because of my father.' Her face fell, she even wept, she embraced me without words, kept me home from school the next day. Then we moved, far from our neighborhood, a new school, new friends, no one knew me, a very lengthy interlude, and then questions, questions…

'Real men are those who shape themselves,' Mama once told me, I translated: 'You aren't your father, don't worry about what he was.' But what was he then? I wanted to know. And surrounding me there was nothing but lifeless eyes!

Did I leave any traces on the beach?

No, the body would certainly have been swept away by the tide, yes, it rises and sweeps everything clean.

My hands, will there be any trace of my hands? Did I leave my imprint on her throat? An indentation, a piece of fingernail, anything that the cops could find. No, they won't find anything, because they're no good and because the sea will wash everything away.

They will find nothing and I'll be able to go back. A kind of escape, just a little getaway they'll say, youth must have its fling. I will see Fati again, maybe in the interim she'll have understood, she'll have realized how lucky she is to be loved. We will cross the deserts that separate us. I will watch her ambitions, she surely will accept my faults. Love is accepting each other, isn't it? I clearly remember one of our first conversations.

'But finally, I don't understand, you have no profession, you aren't studying anymore, you have no aspirations.'

'But of course I have a profession: it's loving you, I'm involved in serious studies: I want to explore every nook of your body and your spirit, I'm aspiring toward something: to staying close to you, always.'

'You can write poetry, I know, but that's not a life. They ask me every day, what does he do, your friend? I have no answer.'

'You don't need to answer, it's very simple. What business is it of theirs? They can clearly see that I don't lack anything.'

'That's it, you lack for nothing because your parents are rich, you think that's a destiny, having nothing but rich parents? And you? How could you not exist by your own doing?'

'You know I'm studying for a diploma.'

'Oh, don't make me laugh. Never at the university, never with a book. You're not preparing yourself for anything at all.'

'Yes I am, every day I'm preparing to wait for you.'

'Oh, you shouldn't hedge, you must look things in the face, you shouldn't... '

'Fati, your phone is ringing.'

'I won't answer it. Me, I believe that in life we ought to find ourselves a purpose, a reason for being, otherwise we're nothing, that's what my father taught me.'

I almost retorted that her father, a great lawyer, a great 'opponent', turned his battle into an easy way of becoming rich. I chose distraction:

'I'm inviting you tonight. A small concert, a very interesting Tuareg group at Océanides, a really nice place by the sea, you'll see, you'll like it.'


Now the sky has freed itself from the black weight and shimmers with its own lights, countless stars winking at the earth. What do they think of us, the stars? Do they see me, are they aware of my woe? I try counting them, quickly give up, and then I forget myself, distance myself, I want to live on a star, I search for one, the biggest one, I concentrate really hard, erase everything, mount an imaginary ray and I rise, I rise, the bad smells recede, a cool wind caresses me, I'm swimming in the firmament of oblivion, but I can't stop imagining the thread breaking, and the fall, the terrible terrifying fall... But no, the ascent stops dead in its tracks, I stay suspended in the air, yes, torn between heaven and earth forever, I'm going to die crucified, a shepherd actually told me once: that star over there is 'the crucified one', Orion, Thamud as they call it, he cut the throat of the camel of Salah the Prophet, and God punished him, eternally suspended, eternally lamenting his lot, between heaven and earth, and his hand is down there, the red star is his hand, the hand of crime, eternally bloodied, making him suffer eternally.

But I don't want to inhabit eternity, suffering forever, I

feel myself trembling, close to weeping, I touch my hand, feel my body, am I still here? Won't the rages of time swallow me whole? Hasn't the star of celestial punishment caught up with me, will I expiate my crime forever? I who believed in nothing just a few hours ago, here I am with my throat dry, hanging on to myths, conquered by the languages of years. I must pull myself together, shake myself, I get up and close my eyes, first I have to belong to myself.

Fall, the cook, has lit a huge fire, his all-white livery coat seems incongruous to me in this space. He's humming to himself. He seems happy. Camels bellow in the distance: the shepherds are returning. In these regions the night is drowsiness, you fall asleep quickly, rocked by the rustling of still lifes, by the always-blue sky, even when it's black, by the gaze of the stars, and by the music of the silence.

Sidi and his friends aren't back yet.


Tomorrow I will go to the city and I will say: 'I'm the one', and all of it will stop, things in their place, I will join my father in the lair of infamy, they will vomit up my name as well. It doesn't matter to me! I see their hideous faces and their voices strangled by the profusion of saliva, droning their false prayer beads, and uttering shapeless words that condemn me and my father all the way back to the first generations. But at least no one will inherit my damnation.

On the other hand, why would I accept their judgments? Why put up with the nasty swipes and keep quiet? Why bow my head and say 'yes' to their hypocritical speeches? Sure, we are assassins, my father and I, but where then are the innocent sheep? Every day, every instant, they suck people's blood, they steal bread from the poor, stuffed into their opulent armchairs they send thousands, if not millions of innocents to their death every minute. And aren't they letting entire populations die of starvation and illness? No, one shouldn't feel too guilty: blood and tears are part of humanity's oldest traditions.

But am I then becoming a monster? Stealing a life? Offering good reasons for murder? She hadn't done anything. She was just too fond of men, and she had a name. That's what I killed, the name. I strangled a sound. Still, she was screaming, first her eyes twitched in bewilderment, then they almost bolted from their sockets, migrating from the hollows that sheltered them, an extreme terror, but all I heard was the dreadful howling of the storm devastating everything inside me, my body, my conscience, everything had vaporized under the furious blows of fate, one name, one name only... The Cheikh.

That name had hurt me in conversations so many times, on the radio, in mosques, it seemed the whole world had agreed to make me hear it. A punishment. The Cheikh, the scholar, the holy man, the sole center of his time, the Cheikh... who dispenses the goods of the here and now and of the beyond, the Cheikh... come from a family of wisdom and piety... the Cheikh... praised day after day in mosques and family homes.

And, in contrast, the Other, the negation of the holy, who dispenses madness, horror, who bears the desolation mark of the new times, the Antichrist, it's he, the vile one, the villain, Satan of recent days. The Other, that was my name, my blood, in some way that was I. What's left of him? Nothing but a feeling of revulsion. 'A crook,' I once heard my mother say in private to one of her women friends, 'a perfect crook, but I can't manage to get him out of my mind, he left his mark on me, the fool, it's crazy how much I loved that brute.' Then, and I don't know why, I felt an immense joy permeating me, 'she loved him once', I've forgotten the rest, 'she loved him', that means he can be loved... So he wasn't a monster... Those words exonerated me from the feeling I'd tried so hard to have for him. I discovered a crack in the very solid wall his detractors presented against him.

But really, why should I be looking for good reasons to love him? Why should I let him infiltrate the already feeble fissures of my life? I don't need his memory, he's nothing to me because he never bent over my cradle, he never took me in his arms, he never wiped the tears from my cheeks. What true bond could possibly unite us? Fatherhood? Isn't that being present? Isn't that love? What did he ultimately bequeath me that I should remember him? Rejection? Exile? A pariah's fate? The tree owes nothing to the peasant who sowed its seed and then abandons it to the stings of sand and wind.

For a long time I hesitated to speak his name, I had trouble uttering the letters that wounded me, that seemed to be full of terrifying threats to me, naming him was tempting dark destinies.

With enormous effort, I once said to my mother: 'My father... ' The words came out of my mouth with difficulty, I was still trying out its sharp and dangerous edges, 'my father'. My mother thought I was talking about her husband: 'Still with his camels, he'll be back in a week.' That was it, the other one no longer existed, he'd vanished from her thoughts, had become a distant ghost made of sorrow and shame. I didn't pursue it.


One day a lecture entitled 'The Cheikh and his contribution to faith' drew my attention, I went there on the sly with a full turban tied around my face as if there were even a chance I might be recognized. I sat in the last row. The speaker was a fairly young man with an olive complexion, a thin face, a brimless head-covering the way pilgrims to Mecca like to wear it, and constantly stroking a beard he apparently thought to still be too short. He spoke about Sufism. I didn't  understand all of it because the terminology was abstruse and the sound system mediocre, but it was clear that it had to do with a form of connecting with God, a desire to dwell in heaven and not be plagued by questions from down here anymore. The Cheikh, he explained, had widely popularized this doctrine and brought it closer to the people. He had many disciples and even performed miracles. The speaker emphasized the last point. He made it clear that God had granted the Cheikh a power inaccessible to ordinary mortals, that he knew how to grasp the mysteries of earth and spirit, that he could understand and explain every phenomenon, just as he knew every thought that people had, everything that crossed their mind, nothing could be kept hidden from him, he knew how to read the book of Creation.

In answering someone's question he broached the circumstances of his death. He explained that it was a conspiracy of the enemies of God, of the atheist West, and of the lackeys of his inner circle. To make this happen they'd selected a man devoid of any compassion who had abandoned him in the desert, him and two of his disciples, had left them to die of thirst and starvation. I almost raised my hand to ask: how could this omniscient spirit, who knows how to access the secrets of things and thoughts, have allowed himself to be led astray into a plan that was going to cause his downfall? Was it suicide or was it a disruption in his machine that made time speak? I stopped myself. Fortunately!

But why have I become a prisoner of someone I do not know, about whom I know nothing, who never took me into his arms, whose beard I never pulled, and who made my mother suffer? Whatever the case may be, today his ghost must be effaced, disappear forever, because I've put an end to my restless wandering beside his shadow. So this must be stopped, like Raya's shrieks the moment I wrung her throat. But those haven't gone silent, I can hear them still...

Tomorrow I will go into the city and I will say: 'It's me.'

They're back. I hear the sound of the motors. Fall has already laid pure white tablecloths on the fine sand, their edges held down by heavy stones. Cushions and place settings are ready. I didn't help him at all. I kept dozing, suspended between dream and reality. My friends' arrival brings me back to everyday life. I have to talk, listen, sometimes laugh. In other words, I have to live, while all of me still floats in the ocean of lifeless horrors.

The children begin to shout as soon as they see me. All three of them dash forward and throw themselves around my neck.

The oldest of the girls is Evelyne, her teeth are darkly stained, her hair is golden, a pretty little storybook face, and a habit of calling me 'Mister greatest storyteller of the Sahara', a nickname Sidi gave me. She thinks it's my real name.

There is little Roger, a tiny boy with long ears; I call him Gavroche because he has an astonishing gift for getting dirty, because nobody in the world can keep him from burying his head in the sand, because he has a mischievous look in his eyes and quick legs, and most of all because he often sings an old revolutionary song that Sidi taught him whose words he doesn't understand at all.

Nathalie has long hair, a small hand-drawn mouth, pink cheeks made to be kissed, she is the sweetest and, I believe, the most intelligent one, she knows how to listen quietly, she knows how to say gentle 'thank you's' all the time, she likes books, she's reserved, she covers her mouth with her hand when she laughs. But her seriousness is countered by eyes that light up with every playful moment.

I've talked about the children because they are my friends. I haven't managed to close the distance with the parents, although they are very civil, they speak to me often and listen to me with interest, but the age difference, the culture perhaps, has created a gap between us that I have never dared cross.

Bruno and Nadine are a couple of teachers, they're about forty. He is lean with a slight belly, a mop of black hair streaked with white, he doesn't speak much, often only shakes his head yes or no, but he certainly knows how to listen and he even takes notes sometimes. His wife is more outgoing, she asks a lot of questions about everything, she takes a lot of pictures, but most of the time she's running after little Roger. Nathalie doesn't cause her any problems.

Johnny and Michelle are a retired couple. He was an English professor and she a juvenile judge. They don't say much to each other but share affectionate glances. I imagine they've had a happy life without too many setbacks. Their children, twins around thirty, male and female, have stayed home. They're in the theater.

Sadi and Marie are Evelyne's parents. He is of Kabyle origin but knows absolutely nothing about Algeria, which he left as a child, and he grew up with his Italian mother. Sidi sometimes calls him 'cousin' and that makes him laugh. Marie is from Besançon, she works in The Restless, a large bookstore, I like that name. Is there anyone more restless than I?

I hardly communicate with the others, both in their fifties, just shake their hands. Maybe they're very introverted and prefer watching nature or meditating in the void rather than talking to a young man who clearly doesn't know anything about anything.

And yet we've spent some wonderful moments on the banks of the Arguin, we've seen a thousand iridescent colors above the ocean, we've admired the millions of birds that come to the island to escape from the rigors of the northern climates, we've seen the Imraguen people launch their fragile rowboats amid the roaring waves, we've danced to the sound of drums and the *med'h*, our form of the blues. It's true that I didn't say a word while we were together, I never joined in their conversations, I simply answered a few questions, in the evenings I mostly spoke with the children, I showed them the stars and told them about the love of Eddebaran and the beautiful Thouraava, and finally I told them a local version of Cinderella, an orphan girl whose jealous stepmother sends her away from home, and who then meets prince charming who marries her and brings her to large tents with golden spears and to summits that kiss the sky, 'later on,' I said, 'I will tell you more stories... '

I have to live up to my promises and am quickly surrounded by the children. They don't forget a thing. I owe them
something. They're having dinner and are watching me in case I
might think of running off. Sidi announced it: I am the Sahara's
best storyteller. Of course, he exaggerates, but I've always been
passionate about legends and stories. I've collected hundreds of
them. It was a griot, a friend of my mother's, who sowed the
seed in me. He knew how to tell stories using Biblical language
and the gestures of a grand lord. The hand movements followed
the melody of the words, he'd sway his head, sometimes fall
silent, then after the silence his words would suddenly emerge,
his whole face bathed by the magic of the ancient myths, as if
his eyes were watching a vanished world that reappeared just
for him alone and whose secrets he wanted to entrust to us. I
dreamed of writing a book on the 'Tales and Legends of the Sahara'.

Fall relit the fires, now a huge inferno. I must silence my
anguish and speak.

I can't find my old stories anymore, they're gone, I chase after
them in my memory but they run away from me, I can't even
get hold of a single snippet although I've spent a lot of time with
them, they inhabited my language for a long time and would
come out in a rapid unconscious flow, I even had them classi-
fied—for children, for adults, for the elderly, for eyes that ask
nothing, for those that gleam with eagerness to live, for idle
spirits, for agile brains, I would regulate their delivery, slow
and somnolent at night, lively in the daytime. But my head and
heart are empty tonight, I cannot find my stories, they've fled,
somewhere, carefully sheltered, I can't find the tiniest shred,
and even the images they convey refuse to come to me, I'm
ashamed, I'm afraid of disappointing those very attentive little

faces, hands on their elbows, forgetting their games, anxious already, waiting for me at the edge of their dreams.

And then I decide to let all of it go, let go of my memory that has abandoned me, create a story for myself, too, that will pour out of me spontaneously, no matter the improbabilities, no matter the contradictions, I would escape myself also, far away, and perhaps I would forget a little.

*'Once upon a time when people were happy, a djinn named Omom, who belonged to the Semar tribe, a tribe of good djinns, who came from the city of Narnar—where did I find all those names?—, an enormous city located right in the center of the vast planet of the good djinns.'*

'What are djinns?'

True, I hadn't thought of it, djinns don't exist in the tales of other people, they're not fairies or ghosts, not zombies, what are djinns?

*'Djinns are creatures like us, they mix with us without being seen, they have their life, we have ours, but they're always with us, at night you can hear them sing with the wind, sometimes they rustle in the trees, they graze on the grass, they live in the forests, in abandoned houses also, but some of them live very far away from us, they hardly ever visit Earth, or only very rarely, those are the best, those are the good djinns.*

*Good djinns are creatures like us, which means that they have bodies and minds, but their bodies are formless and their minds know only good, they have fathers and mothers but they grow up very fast, only a few hours after they're born, just  like some animals, but they aren't animals at all.'*

'What are they?'

'Good djinns, that's all.'

*Good djinns don't have any homes but they don't need*

them, they don't wear any clothes, they don't need them, they're wrapped in glass, a kind of glass that for us is impossible to imagine and so also impossible to describe, they don't know what sleep is, they don't know what fatigue is, they don't need cars or planes; they wander around free in their gracious city. They drink the fine air and it fills them up, they're unfamiliar with the damaging effects of bad smells and pollution, they don't know suffering, they don't grow old, they just evaporate when they've lived too long, they vanish just like that into the atmosphere, like incense, a white aromatic smoke, they don't go to school but they never stop learning or being amazed because the good djinns are eternal children and they study every day and know an impressive number of things, they don't know anger or jealousy or hate, they pray to God to never wear the defects that all too often inhabit the Earthlings; I said 'they pray' but that's only a manner of speaking because good djinns don't really have a religion. They love life, they love what's beautiful, they detest lies and injustice.

The good djinns live in a city full of poetry; you can't understand this because the difference between our world and that of the djinns is too great. For us, poetry is words that carry beautiful images and trace beautiful lines in hearts and minds. In the world of the good djinns poetry is a living matter with which homes are built, poetry is a matter with which large avenues are built where views get lost. Poetry is produced by the surrounding stars, by the sky that waters them, by the planets that turn as they sing, by distant seas and retreating lands, by loves that find shelter in gazing eyes. So it is a bounteous matter that they use to treat the heart and to build realms of dreams.

But there aren't any trees in the town of the good djinns, no mountains in their country, no sea, the landscape is nothing but small and big stars, the countless little ones shimmer and you see them everywhere as they wander freely through the city. Sometimes the good djinns mount them for a ride in the sky or, less often, to go to another planet, but not to ours because I assure you they don't like to come to Earth, they say that it's too far and that *it's a planet inhabited by conceited people who have no reason at all to be that way because they fight and don't like each other, because they torment nature and live under the influence of their worst enemies, the bad djinns. These bad djinns live on a planet different from the one of our friend Omom but they conquered our Earth a long time ago and laid siege to the hearts and minds of its inhabitants, you don't see these bad djinns but they're always around us whispering in our ears and our hearts, they make us tell lies, they make us hate, they make us do bad things.*

'What's the planet of the bad djinns called?'

'It doesn't have a name because they hide.'

'Why do they hide?'

'Precisely because they are bad.'

*As I was saying, in the land of the good djinns, the little stars are like taxis but they're free, everyone can use them; as for the large planets, those are places where you can go on vacation, just as you are doing here. Over there you have beaches of ice and beaches of fire, I say 'ice' and 'fire' but don't think it's hard to live in those places, no, it's like the beach is for us, they dive into it, they fish in it, and discover fabulous subterranean worlds in it; the fire is like springtime here, an entrancing display of colors that we wouldn't be able to tell apart from permanent fireworks, plays of light that never end, magical landscapes.*

*The good djinns have no police, no army and no government, they don't need them because deep inside themselves there is no jealousy, no pride, no one steals from anyone else, no one attacks anyone else, there aren't even any laws because the law is inside people's head. There is only an assembly, a few good djinns selected at random, who know how to listen and who give their opinion when asked. That assembly is called the Heart.*

*So in that land of good djinns lived a young man named Omom. He was a curious boy, in love with life, his head full of songs and poetry. He loved his planet very much, he felt hap-*

py there, he breathed the scent of beautiful things and good
people there, but he also dreamed of seeing other places. I said
'dreamed' but dreams don't exist among the good djinns, even
wanting had but little power because the good djinns had just
about everything they desired. But Omom was special and everybody knew it. Traveling, as I told you, was a very common
custom of the good djinns, they moved around the universe as
they chose, but Omom didn't want to do what the others did, he
didn't want to visit from afar, he wanted to get close to humans,
speak with them, live like them, grasp their truths. However, the
good djinns knew everything already, in their minds they had
stored all the knowledge of the distant planets. But that knowledge wasn't enough for Omom, he was dreaming of touching life,
of being clad in it.

Above all he was dreaming of the very peculiar planet they
call Earth. He'd read everything about it, he knew its population
was dense, ingenious, conceited, he knew that they liked slaugh-
tering and kissing each other, that they liked lying and shouting
truths, that they were very poor and very rich at the same time,
that they'd invent each day, would create their own nature every
morning and destroy it every moment, and that they could cultivate in themselves the strongest loves and the most irrational
hates.

He also knew that the Earthlings were heavily influenced
by the bad djinns who prodded them to tell lies, be traitors, and
wage war. The bad djinns appointed kings and queens down
there, established empires, eroded the body and mind of the
Earthlings but they, and he found that astonishing, didn't all fall
under the absolute influence of the bad djinns, some of them, a
small minority, still had enough heart to refuse the dictat, few in
number, true, but Omom thought it was marvelous that there
still were men and women on that dark and deformed planet
who didn't cave in under the weight of the wicked spirits.

So Omom decided to go to Earth. Many of the good djinns
thought his project was peculiar. It was enough to see that plan-

*et from afar, a round desolate ball from which no light emerged at all floating in the middle of an ocean of nothingness. The few good djinns who'd gone there a very, very long time ago had come back nauseated. Omom insisted. He would go to our planet.'*

What else should I come up with as encounters, adventures? It's a long time ago that I read *The Little Prince*, I forgot the details. Besides, the children must know anyway. I'm feeling tired, the anguish is rising in my heart again and my imagination has stopped speaking.

'Children,' I say, 'for tonight I'll stop here and I'll pick up the story again tomorrow, I want you to sleep, to have sweet dreams, to kiss your moms, and patiently wait for the rest.'

Some small grunts but my desertion was accepted. They were actually exhausted, they must have run around all day through the sands, were already yawning a little.

They left again and I refused to go along with them. Sidi insisted a lot, the children clung to me, as did their parents or almost, but I said no, I know Terjit; and its palm trees filled with water leaning over the edge of a source that never runs dry, and those mountains that have been threatening to collapse for millennia without ever taking the final step. Terjit is a mess, an atom of water and coolness molded inside a hollow mountain in the middle of a desert of regs, dunes, and starving palm trees, a paradise for tourists and well-fed citizens. The children will romp around in the water, the adults will doze all day in a cave of happiness, contemplating the drops that flow from green stalactites counting time, sheltered from the sky's fire by monsters of stone; Terjit is a fraud, all around for hundreds of kilometers nothing but mountains of fire, white sand and the biting hot wind, and there's a minuscule oasis to make you forget the oppressive barrenness of the entire region. Terjit is a hypocrisy of nature.

I feel immense hate toward all lies and all forms of hypocrisy today. Everywhere you go, people show us which path to follow, books, sayings, newspapers bombard us with obvious truths, and with their actions those who imprison our minds lie and pillage every day, steal from us, and we nod our head, accepting the nonsense they feed us. Why was the Cheikh a holy man and my father a thug? Do people look into the heart of others, into what stirs them? Does morality exist, does it still have any meaning, did it ever? Why have I always felt ashamed of being my father's son and by what ploy should Raya be proud of hers?

And Fati, isn't she all lies? Why did she drop me if it weren't for the lies? She was thinking of what people might say about her, she was thinking about her father's career, and perhaps she hadn't even loved me anymore for a long time either? When the press gets hold of the case she'll become very small, she'll be afraid to see her name displayed in the news, but no, it won't be you they'll see, nobody will remember you, it's me alone they'll send to hell, yes, hell that's what I am predestined for, but I swear to you, I really did love you, yes, before my heart dried up I truly loved you. Today I'm completely black inside and I don't know how to love anything anymore.

I can see the headlines on the electronic sites and that newspapers must already be showing: 'The daughter of the great Cheikh found murdered', 'Who killed the holy man's daughter?', 'Murder on the beach, killer at large'. And later, once they've found me: 'The story continues: the son of the thug strangles the daughter of the holy man...', 'Criminal from father to son...'. They'll paint an evil portrait of me, they'll search, they'll find an image where I'll appear as a malicious and dangerous idiot and they'll show Raya, very pure, an innocent round face, an honest, modest girl from a good family. Who are they to differentiate the chosen from the fallen? Sure, I'll grant that I'm nothing, a nasty mold, but they, what are they really, do they know what lies down there within me?

In any event, it won't take them long to effortlessly fill

their columns. Tomorrow I'll go back to the city and I'll say: 'It's me.'

Haven't the police gone after me yet? No, it's still too early but as soon as they recognize the body there will be a general reaction, consternation. I know Commissioner Dahoud, he's a friend of my mother's, he's been at the house several times, meticulously elegant but with the head of a minor clerk, malicious eyes all the same, an investigator, that's obvious. He's constantly looking everywhere, all around him and into people's eyes, once I heard him talk about a murder he'd managed to solve in just one day, he said, merely boasting I thought. Nevertheless, everybody thinks he's a good policeman and a helpful man. He will certainly be the one to deal with the affair, the beach is in his sector I believe. But what will they find? A lifeless body at the edge of the sea, no witnesses, no traces. I'm sure I didn't leave any footprints. Maybe there are tracks in the sand, but the wind will have quickly wiped them away. Have they even discovered the body yet? How soon will they find it? That part of the beach is very rarely visited by anyone, almost never, except on weekends. And besides, the sea must have risen and swallowed it all, high tide removes everything.

But it's certain that the disappearance of the Cheikh's daughter will bring everyone together. They'll be looking for her everywhere. They'll be questioning her friends... but I've never been one of her friends.

She honked loudly when I passed her. In the rearview mirror I noticed that waving arm ordering me to stop. The traffic was moving very well that afternoon. She pulled her car over next to mine. She was wearing huge sunglasses that covered half her face and a pendant that slipped down between her breasts. What did we say?

'Oh, it's you,' she said, 'I was waiting for your call but it never came.'

'No, I did try but I wrote down the number incorrectly.'

"Liar! It's because you weren't in any hurry to see me, that's all.'

'Not true, it would be madness not to want to get together with a girl like you.'

'You men are all the same: little lies and compliments.'

'No, I assure you and besides Isma told me... '

I don't remember anymore what I had Isma say.

'You have any time?'

'Yes, why?'

'To talk, to chat, to get to know each other better?'

'A cup of coffee?'

'Yes.'

'At the Sahara?'

'No, too many people there.'

'The beach then?'

'The beach.'

She might not have accepted, I might not have run into her... It would have taken nothing for us to keep on living a little.

Minou, the camel driver, came over and knelt down beside me, he has the unceremonious ways of the nomads, and thinks it's his duty to talk to me.

'You slept a long time, you must be very tired.'

I don't answer, look elsewhere. It doesn't seem to bother him.

'The well of our wadi has collapsed. From now on we'll

have to go farther to look for water. But the best thing would be to dig another well, it'll cost a lot because we'll have to dig very deep, ah yes, my dear friend, the water is escaping, sinking deeper and deeper into the ground, it has to do with the drought, but also with the evil eye, it's true, the people in the region were always jealous of the clarity and flavor of our water, they would always say: "Such water! Such water!" There you have it, do you think your friends could help us?'

'Which friends?'

'The foreigners, of course.'

'They're not my friends.'

'But you could...'

'I can do nothing for you.'

'Excuse me, I forgot, you're from the city, you're all the same, no solidarity with anything.'

He gets up waving his arms around. I'm glad to be rid of him. These nomads don't understand that one might want to be alone. That's because they all too often are. And besides, they despise all that's urban, I know what they say: 'The city is for slaves, for the worthless, and for domestic animals.' They're so selfish... I don't know what my adoptive father sees in them, arrogant and dirty, that's what they are.

But what am I saying? No, the sea couldn't rise that high, impossible, the body will remain visible on the beach, but at this time of year that area isn't visited a lot. Still, it's certain some people will come. And what about the fisherman, the one we saw in the distance, he must have seen something. Traces, those they will find. There's DNA as well, and that's irrefutable. The two of us also went across the city, someone must have seen us. And when we got to the beach, I carried her in my arms, do imprints become embedded in clothes, on bodies? Of course, they'll find me. Never mind! I'll go to the city tomorrow in any case and I'll tell them everything.

It will be devastating for my mother, an entire edifice she had patiently constructed that will suddenly fall into ruins. She wanted to delete the hated name, recreate an honest ancestry for me. A new birth certificate first of all. Not the despised name, she used my grandfather's name and then the one of my extended family, a way of confusing the issue without cutting the obvious bridges. She abandoned me to the arms of my grandmother and then she really had to take me back, send me to a good school, protect me from the ghosts of the past. What will she do tomorrow? I don't dare imagine her reaction. She'll scream, roll around on the ground. No, instead she'll appear rather unperturbed, with clenched face and lips she will display an admirable serenity in the face of adversity, she won't say a word, but invisible lava will flow deep inside her heart.

It's my father's sister who was the first to trouble the serene framework my mother had erected, the taboo that ruled the house: my father's name was not to be uttered, ever. I was already fourteen years old when she came to see us, she demanded to take me with her for a few days' vacation. Mama tried to resist, but my aunt was ready to stir up the whole city, shout around that they refused to let her have her nephew, her blood, something my mother feared above all. Still, she gave a thousand reasons to keep me from going, I had extra classes to take, I needed special care, I suffered from asthma, but my aunt persevered. They came to an agreement that my aunt disclosed to me afterward: I would stay just one week and no one would speak to me about my father. Actually, my mother thought that my aunt lived in a distant village, that she had no connection with our kind of people and that 'this wouldn't become known'. She called me several times a day to make sure 'everything was going well'.

Anyway, my aunt didn't talk about the criminal act that hauled my father off to prison and into disgrace, she simply evoked the image of a handsome man, generous, intelligent, adventurous, a poet who loved life. A poet, that set my mind on fire, my father, a poet, I had just discovered my first poems, I loved Mahmoud Darwish and Victor Hugo. My father, my real father as she said, was a great poet, it made me shiver. Instantly I enhanced him with new colors. She recited one of his poems for me, not the most successful one by any means:

> *On that national holiday*
> *I did not see the troops parade*
> *I did not hear the cannon thunder*
> *I did not hear the anthem sung*
> *I did not see the women adorned*
> *I did not see the crowds in song*
> *I did not hear any speeches*
> *I did not see the flag be raised*
> *I only saw Mariem who smiled*
> *And I felt my heart that wept*

Ah, when I think about it today, I could well have been the writer of that poem, yes, if I had a little talent I could have written it for Fati. Yes, I saw her from afar that day, she was talking with someone, her hands were moving, like this, her face was sullen but beautiful, small arms escaped from a fine veil that also showed a lock of hair covering the upper part of her forehead, she seemed worried, she was speaking with fervor it appeared, and then she turned around and signaled to someone, then her face lit up, her eyes sent something like a challenge, I instinctively stretched out my arm as if to hold on to the moment, she turned her back to me and dove into a car that was waiting for her. I asked about her. 'Fati,' I was told, 'is the daughter of a famous attorney, deputy of the opposition, she is with her father at every demonstration, she has a degree, at meetings she often takes the floor, she has a great future.' I swore to myself that I would see her again.

So that's it, my father and I have gone through the same thing, we were thrown into the same turmoil, the same torment, we are alike, he is somewhere inside me. No he's not, he's more of a wanderer, he knows how to forget, erase everything and write new poems, while I remain a prisoner of motionless visions. And besides I've never hurt anyone. Never hurt anyone? What about Raya, lying lifeless on the edge of an ocean of tears?

It's hot in the tent Sidi pitched for me, a very flimsy shelter where the inquisitive looks of a sun that knows how to gain access sneak in everywhere, I haven't eaten yet but I'm not hungry, the dry bread, the cookies, and even the gamey meat never left the silver tray, a supreme luxury in this sterile environment. I am thirsty, however, they've taken away the huge thermoses full of ice and the containers of water. Outside on the lower branches of a tree with faded leaves hangs the goatskin swaying in a feeble wind. Outside a leaden sun welcomes me, Irivi's wind, this land's burning breath, batters my face, mirages dance in the distance. Why do they give themselves to me who no longer dreams of an oasis?

Does Isma know that we left together? Impossible, our meeting was unexpected and we didn't contact anyone, I think. My cell phone rang once, it was Mama, I didn't pick up. Raya had forgotten her phone in her car, she tried to call someone with mine but the call didn't go through, 'that damned system', she said.

They're certainly in the process of investigating now, looking for clues, questioning everyone. What could Isma possibly tell them? She is the only one, I believe, who knows both of us.

They must have found Raya's car, her cell phone, they'll check her call history. Had she already listed my number? Isma must have given it to her. I don't know, but there have to be hundreds of names listed in her contacts.

Isma works at the administration, she's even a department head, only twenty-three years old, that's because her father is very influential, a former minister or something like that, her mother is a woman who carries her weight as well, in every sense of the word, she's a shopkeeper, runs a luxury boutique. You should see Isma with her family or at the office, a virtuous creature, showing only her face, her head always lowered, speaking in half-words, language full of clichés, barely moving, a respectful well-born young woman. You should see her at our parties, her hair all messy, arrogant in her speech, a birdbrain, a fast girl, railing against every prohibition. How does she manage to play both characters, I have never been able to play a single true role.

I showed my father's photograph to a few of my friends without saying anything, just 'what does this man inspire in you?' Some shrugged their shoulders, nothing, others said: 'Not a bad guy, he likes the fast life, that's for sure,' yes, he had real joie de vivre, he'd laugh with his head back, his hair ruffled, a turban around his neck that came down to his waist and that he held casually with one hand, very white teeth, a broad smile, Mama was next to him, arms crossed, almost unrecognizable, her face somewhat out of focus, but she wasn't laughing. Who took that photo? I don't know, but it's certainly old, I couldn't have been born yet, it was crumpled and part of it was slightly worn, but then I knew: he didn't look like an assassin, everyone thought he was handsome and kind. It was my aunt, his sister, who showed it to me, I quickly shoved it in my pocket, hid it from my mother. I looked at it for hours, I wanted to read his soul in it, penetrate it and by looking at him I felt him come to other people say, he was not an assassin.

I'm hearing the sound of a motor. It's not my friends, the car is coming from the wrong direction, still it seems to be heading our way. Other tourists perhaps? But Sidi is the only one who has clients at this time and in this place. Are they coming to get me? I shudder, fear seeps into me, pierces me with its stings, I try to resist but the torrent is strong. They're coming to destroy me, deliver me to the howling beasts, they will spit in my face, eat my flesh and my bones, they will put me on view in the public square, a monster, son of a monster, a sinner, son of a sinner, they will burn my body and refuse to put me into the earth in order to once and for all kill off the seeds that inhabit me, a wandering soul without a grave, I will be smoke that will fly off into the atmosphere to fade away forever.

I try to pull myself together and must stay clear-headed I tell myself. Why should I panic? I had to know they would find my traces anyway. Today nobody can disappear anymore or obliterate the signs of their presence, we are spotted everywhere, every touch, every step, every movement leaves a signal behind, our footprints, our genes, everything inside us screams and struggles, prisoner of a minuscule chip, our entire life is in their hands, how could I possibly disappear like this and get away from them?

The noise grows louder, they're coming closer. I try to control myself again, I have to pay my debts, I must suffer the punishment, I have taken a life, I must pay for it with my own, it's fair, I try to manage the all too strong impulses of my body but the panic in me rises and my body becomes a smoking haze, my innards begin to wail.

The car stops and I hear someone calling, 'anyone here, anyone here', I don't move, I wouldn't know how to walk or say a word without betraying myself. I hear Minou talking to them, I listen but can't make out the voices. Right away the engine starts up again, I feel an enormous weight has been lifted from me.

My aunt had placed a rather idyllic portrait of my father before me. He was a man with a big heart, she said, who loved people and especially his own, loved her, loved his sister who had died, and loved their mother, he'd helped them a lot, he'd started working at a very early age so they wouldn't fall into poverty, for the drought had devastated all their cattle, wasted away under the blows of the Saharan sun, three years without any rain, and they were left without anything, so they fled their camps to go to the city and he had slaved away to provide the essentials.

I now know that at first he was involved in smuggling, he had merchandise brought in across borders that belonged to big traders and he knew how to take risks. Then he befriended some powerful figure and took care of his immense herd, hundreds of camels. He rediscovered his old nomadic genes and he loved that life, following the clouds' traces everywhere, going wherever there was growing grass. The super-wealthy political man ended up getting into trouble and selling all his cattle, but my father refused to work with the new owner, and became a guide and an adventurer of the great outdoors, there was no one better than he to travel around with tourists, to find a lost flock, to bring missing city dwellers back to far-off camps, to forge an improbable path in the immense jumble of dunes and deserts of pebbles and stones.

Why would a man like he, so blissful in the middle of empty spaces, so little interested in today's commodities, go on to break the thread of his life? I wanted to know, I couldn't expect anything from my mother who would wrap herself in fearful silence, from my aunt I would only get snippets of stories, and besides I now know that she had initially dissociated herself from him and that it wasn't until later, after his death, that she felt a kind of remorse and found the courage to defend him. It is clear that the Cheikh's aura tethers minds, that the version reported by those close to him had been repeated so often, defended by the religious scholars, the press, the politicians and even the poets, that it had become inscribed on the people's tongues and in their conscience. I suspected that this wall of unanimity was too tightly woven to let any clarifications through. I wanted to know. That thirst had grabbed me by the throat and wouldn't let go anymore.

I went to visit the old archives of the newspaper *Chaab*, the important daily of the time. I knew I didn't have much chance of finding any articles of the past. In that era the press only offered interminable editorials glorifying the Leader.

At the door of an old-fashioned building I was received by an employee wearing a jacket of an unidentifiable color over a still-blue boubou. With a nonchalant gesture of the hand he directed me to the archives office. Relegated to the back of a dark hallway it reeked of yellowed paper from the moment I stepped in. A woman well in her forties was too occupied with her cell phone to notice my presence. I had to cough loudly before she raised her head.

'What is it you want?'

A bit disconcerted, I almost turned back.

'The archives,' I stammered.

'What archives?'

'Well, the old newspapers.'

'From which period?'

"From about twenty years ago, I think.'

'So you're not sure?'

I didn't know what to say. Actually, I was starting to get scared. Not of her but of the desire to know, which is what brought me here. Why want to dust off time? Do we know what fate time might have in store for us?

'Where do you come from?'

The question troubled me a little. I didn't understand the reason for it.

'I am a student,' I answered, nevertheless.

'Oh fine, so it's for a thesis topic then. Students do come here, but they don't stay long because they find nothing, just bla-bla-bla. Well, you'll see.'

She showed me a spacious room that I entered with muffled steps. It was empty.

'Do you have any headlines, dates? Because, believe me, here there's only what we publish ourselves and even then several copies have disappeared.'

'I don't know exactly... '

'You think I'll know if you don't?'

'Let's say 1998? Just at the beginning of the summer.'

'Ah, that was a booming period, I was the private secretary of the general manager at the time. Bonuses came raining down and visitors even gave me presents sometimes, you see, my friend. They had to in order to be announced right away, ah yes, that's all over now, I'm confined to this revolting hole, I have to say that at that time... '

I couldn't hear the rest very well, she dropped several binders in front of me. I began to flip through them. More often than not they were only official declarations and paeans by the then-president, I slowly turned the pages, was trembling a bit, as if I were going to find myself face to face with my father in the middle of some narrow alleyway. Certain articles that had nothing to do with my father were of interest to me, I forgot myself a little. I was drawn to a weekly column 'Wink of an eye', which used satire to lay into the elite, I skimmed reportages on the ancient desert towns. I wasn't in any rush, I tried to quickly read anything that seemed readable, I was actually afraid to see my father's face appear as I turned a page and was postponing that moment. The woman brought me a cup of tea and a small bottle of mineral water. Her attentiveness surprised me and I uttered a timid 'thank you'. A cheap perfume wafted through the room then faded away. I sighed. Suddenly an image hit me in the face, it was the Cheikh, yes, there he was, the same photo had been plastered on the wall the day I'd gone to the lecture, I stopped breathing, the name was clearly there in huge letters. 'The country has just lost one of its most illustrious religious scholars. The Cheikh was known for his great erudition and his extreme piety. He had countless followers in this country and beyond. With him an extremely valiant spirit has vanished. Our souls belong to God and to Him they shall return. On this sorrowful occasion... ' That's all. Not a word about the circumstances of his death, nothing about my father. I stopped to think, 'why only this morbid press release?' Perhaps on that day they hadn't accused my father yet. Or perhaps the government wanted to avoid any demonstrations by the Cheikh's faithful, or perhaps they didn't know yet how he had died. Moved by an unconscious reflex I suddenly got up from the chair then immediately sat back down again. Had the archivist noticed my agitation? She came toward me and handed me a sheet of paper, 'name, profession, time of visit', I wrote down my full name. She took back the paper, read it out loud, gave me a smile and went back to her desk. I stared at the photo of the Cheikh, he was wearing two boubous, white and blue, one on top of the other and over them a djellaba; his head was covered by a long black turban that hid his chin and mouth but his eyes, you had to see his eyes, they radiated a marvelous glow, a fire, the fire of holiness or enthusiasm. Sometimes the two merge. I looked around, pricked up my ears then tore the page from the paper and quickly stuffed it in my pocket. As I left I put my hands together with a big smile and with a nod of the head I said goodbye to the nice lady, which seemed to please her.

Why wasn't I able to extinguish the inferno inside myself? Why were my attempts at evasion merely passing escapades? I want peace to engulf me, the torments inside me to cease. I, too, want to live a story-life, a journey cradling me, and with my eyes closed, caressed by a gentle sun, listening to the twitter of birds, the song of rustling palm trees, the wind whispering so softly it won't wake me, and through my closed eyelids see beaming nymphs dance.

We didn't really stop at Atar, just long enough for me to park my car in front of the house of one of Sidi's friends. I didn't object. Even though I really felt like slipping into the casbah's old passageways, rediscovering some of my steps, breathing in images and memories but, I told myself, it would be too painful, nothing is the way it used to be, and besides, someone might recognize me and point their finger at me. In addition, I would interrupt the program that Sidi and his friends had so meticulously put together. But I'm still attached to that town, for it's where I spent my early childhood, sent away by a mother who didn't want the signs of a shattered love and a now accursed name by her side any longer. It was here that I lived the only truly happy moments of my life, pampered by a generous and carefree grandmother, running through the casbah's narrow streets, joining the drums and the rugged voices of the *med'h* singers at night, the music of the enslaved that calls upon God and makes people's hearts quaver.

I cried a lot when my grandmother died because I was very close to her, but also because I sensed that everything around me was going to fall apart. And my mother came that very evening, just one single night, to pray at my grandmother's grave and take me away.

My mother never showed the slightest interest in the town where she was born. She never speaks of Atar or of the years of her youth when she lived there. And yet the city left a significant mark on her, she spent her first twenty years there, and it was there that she met my father. But one might say that Atar is a wrinkle she wants to remove. She left it in the arms of a passionate and fickle love and never went back. Maybe she's still ashamed to admit her defeat? The people of Atar would look at her with compassion: 'There's the girl who left on the arm of an adventurous Bedouin and now she's coming back, poor thing, prisoner of his depravities.' For my mother Atar is perhaps an admission of failure, a kind of capitulation, the painful memory of her sorrowful disgrace.

We stopped at the gates of Chinguetti, the city of the old mosque and of dusty manuscripts. I won't go wandering through the alleys here. Sidi really insisted but I said no. I don't like historical towns, I have enough trouble with my present. I'll feel cramped in the mazes of the ancient town, the smell of antique documents will smother me, and I am too turned inward right now to show any interest in the old things I already know. I can recite the phrases Sidi will reel off word for word: 'This city was created in the tenth century, it was an oasis, a meeting place of pilgrims coming from the Sahara and elsewhere in Africa on their way to Mecca, it was prosperous and had I don't know how many ulemas, how many libraries...' I know the instant, the very comma when he'll stop, when he will look his clients in the eye, when he will lower his voice before raising it again, and to impress them even more will bring out a very old book from the librarian's all too well-organized drawers. It is written on gazelle skin dating back a thousand years, useless because it is illegible, and a Bible that a passing Israelite forgot there, all of this to impress the visitors so that everywhere they go they'll sing the praises of Chinguetti's mysteries. Also, it's not very nice for the city and its inhabitants to have the glories of bygone days so eloquently described, it makes too prominent a display of their decline.

Raya said something that outraged me at first, when we were walking to the beach she spoke of, yes, of 'those who're seeking an identity', yes, speaking about Isma she said, 'she's searching for herself', and 'she wants to create an identity as well'. Was this 'as well' directed at me? I know that Isma's grandfather was a *znagui,* a herd watcher, and that in the eyes of the Sahara people that was a low-grade job, but why the 'as well'? Did she know that when my mother authenticated my identity papers she'd ignored the name of my accursed father? Did she already know whose son I was? No, in that case she would surely not have agreed to come with me. Or maybe she knew and wanted to taunt destiny, find a new kind of sensation, or simply provoke her own people? 'Look, I'm the girlfriend of the son of my father's assassin now', one way of throwing sand in the eyes of every one of her father's faithful followers who, she told me, pester her every day. Girls today sometimes have strange ideas.

Sidi set up his camp on a stony terrain a few miles from the town. His friends are too tired now to tackle the high dunes. The smiling hospitality of the town's hotels don't appeal to them either. From afar Chinguetti looks like a mirage from which the dark rooftop of the old mosque emerges; but when you turn your head, the brash installations of the telecommunication companies are an insult to anyone's dreams. Sidi laughs about it: 'Just don't look that way.'

I pitch my tent separately. My isolation is now accepted. Sidi tried hard to speak to me about it: 'Hey, is something wrong, are you sick, are you having some serious problems?' I blamed my state on my old migraines.

Raya's face now appears to me above the towers, it will supplement the invisible signals to scream into the ears of all cell phone subscribers: 'He killed me...'. I try to control my emotions so I won't risk going crazy. In reality, I tell myself, nothing new has happened on a global scale. At any given moment the whole world is nothing but crime. Even where we are, stories of murder fill the newspaper columns and websites. So why be anxious about a news item even if I'm its creator, maybe quite in spite of myself? I might escape from it and in a while it will all be forgotten. I raise my head and look around again. Sidi has put a tube of aspirin beside my bed and a container full of water.

How many crimes in our country remain unsolved? Very few, I think. I've not heard about any murders whose perpetrators weren't discovered. They say that the police have infiltrated the mafia circles to such a degree that they always succeed in identifying the criminals. I've heard Commissioner Dahoud brag to my mother about his accomplishments. Nothing has ever escaped him. How could I even hope to slip through his net?

Of course, he always pursued true criminals, moving in an environment of criminals, having criminal motives, his entire experience, his entire psychology is geared toward that. Finding me, identifying me, would be more taxing. First off, he would consider it a heinous killing. After all, she's a daughter of affluent people, and the fact that they'd find her purse untouched would be meaningless. Besides, they could have stolen a fortune from her. Then, too, since he knows me slightly and associates with my family, he'd brush aside any suspicion of guilt where I'm concerned.

And Fati? What would she think? That she did well by leaving me? Of course! But she will not speak about me, she won't say a word, to her I'm dead, deleted from her memory, she'll even deny having known me, I imagine that to those who saw us together she'll only say: 'Oh no, he did hang around me a bit, certainly, but that's all.' I feel like going back and yelling in her face: 'And what about our laughter that would shake the cold silence from the walls, and our hugs and kisses that revived our flesh of dormant passions, and those poems, taken from an old collection I was writing to you on notebook paper:

*You are an ocean of dreams for my insomniac desire*

*You are the oasis I see from afar, astray,*
*lost in the infinitude of thirsts*
*You are my blood that I feel dancing every instant*
*You are my tribe, the homeland of my only passion*

Do you remember? And I, ready to offer you the world although I had nothing to give, isn't that true? No, better not tell her anything, forget her in fact, not let her be victorious again, it's very difficult but it is bound to pass, I must remain respectable. Tomorrow, when I'll be telling the whole story, everything will be wiped out, even her image, because that's when I shall confront only my own existence, there will be room only for my father and me.

But perhaps I should wait before throwing myself to the wolves? My mother will make it her duty to save me, my adoptive father will spend millions for me not to be accused at all. And besides, isn't Commissioner Dahoud a family friend? And afterward, when I escape the torments I swear that I'll run away, I'll make a new life for myself, I'll follow another path just to forget everything else. Ah yes, I'll emigrate for sure, far away to a Western country, I won't need to throw myself into the arms of ravenous seas, it's only outcasts who use the waters of hunger and despair, I'll get a quick visa, I'll study, get degrees, work, forget my father, and Fati, and the rest.

But none of that manages to calm my inner demons. I know, Dahoud will make it a point of honor to solve this murder, he thinks he's Hercule Poirot, he's fond of his image as a hunting dog, he'll explore every detail, he'll dissect every hypothesis, he'll look at everything, he'll make sure he has ears everywhere. And in the end, he'll exult as he presents my head to his admiring superiors, to the people. No, the friendship with my parents won't matter, he's too devious, too infatuated with himself to spurn a trophy that would be added to his collection of heroics. He'll speak of 'justice' although only arrogance makes him act.

But, after all, what difference does it make to me whether he knows or not? In any case, tomorrow I'll go into the city and I'll say: 'It's me, I did it', 'Assassin, assassin's son!' they'll say. What do I care! I won't even defend myself!

But even if I did kill, maybe at the end of the day I'm only a poor victim, maybe I only inherited a criminal virus. Yes, there are quite a few scientists who've confirmed that crime is transmitted through the genes, that there is a specific criminal type, it's been written up in many books, there were even drawings of predestined assassin's mugs, true I don't have strong jaws, prominent eyebrows, I'm not insensitive to pain, so I don't answer to the descriptions of that Mr. Lombroso who wrote a whole book on the subject. Besides, I don't believe that anyone today follows this thesis any longer, all the same maybe he was right after all, just took a wrong turn when describing a born-killer 'type' while the inheritance isn't physically visible but lies in the mental area or in the chromosomes, the DNA, which in his time wasn't known.

And yet, my aunt definitely told me that it wasn't he, that they had amassed a mountain of false evidence against him, and what's more that there were no witnesses. She didn't dwell on the circumstances of the Cheikh's death. I even think she'd forgotten everything, 'my memory,' she said, 'my head is drained, everything is scrambled inside, there's a crack in there and the memories seep out'. Perhaps she just didn't want to hold on to any morbid memories?

If my father were innocent that would change everything, it's destiny that would have avenged itself by my intervention, yes, maybe I'm only the innocent hand of an invisible force that decreed the death of the Cheikh's daughter? In that case it would be justice that they do not get to me.

I see her now running to the beach in front of me, swinging her bag, she's taken off her veil and uncovered her short hair, a dress that reaches down to her knees tightly hugs her luscious shape, her shaking behind, and I hear her laughter, it still rings in my ears that laughter, she drops down on the sand, she's not afraid to get wet, she's not afraid, she opens her arms to me, I'm a little embarrassed, there's a man in the distance and the sea is wholly present but she's afraid of nothing, we embrace, I'm still looking in the direction of the fisherman I see over there, 'don't worry,' she tells me, 'there's never anyone on the beach at this hour, and besides I'm well protected, you know, I am the Cheikh's daughter...'. 'The false Cheikh', I said just like that without thinking, and her hand came crashing across my cheek, and that's when something inside me shrieked.

A volcano roared. The hidden fire spewed forth. I had gone crazy. I don't remember anything anymore except for that soft body still clinging to me, and those round eyes still wide with astonishment, fixed on the unthinkable horror and on a hideous grin. What did I look like at that moment? A terrifying monster, for sure, she must have screamed. Oh no, it wasn't an avenging spirit that had spoken, it was merely my genes, my evil genes that suddenly leapt out. Oh, I hate the father who bequeathed me nothing but an abhorrent name and its accompanying madness.

Will Dahoud and his cops get to me? How? They would draw up a list of every one of Raya's acquaintances, I believe. My name wouldn't appear on it. Theoretically nobody knows that we were together that day. And then, too, the circle of Raya's acquaintances is certainly very wide, her father's followers are plentiful. Their villa is always full of people, even after the Cheikh was gone. They come to feel the blessings, they bring offerings. She must be getting gifts from everywhere. That's certainly the environment the police will check out first. Perhaps they'll think of a student who is disgusted by her loose behavior, she who in the eyes of a number of the faithful should have been a saint. Perhaps a thug who… But she wouldn't have gone to the beach with a thug.

And if, despite everything, my name were to be mentioned? They'd certainly think about contacting me. And they would realize that I have disappeared. Maybe it's my mother who would alert them in spite of herself. She'd be worried, she'd be afraid for me and call the cops, then the suspicions would begin. There's nothing more suspicious than people. Should I call my mother, tell her I'm with Sidi and will be back soon, and that she shouldn't tell anyone? No, and besides I've already destroyed my cell phone.

And then, my resolve is made, I will pay my debt, I will confess my crime.

Sidi came into my tent, sat down cross-legged, and lit his pipe of *meneja*, a steel tube expertly crafted and embellished by a skillful blacksmith. His pipe is his pride and when you ask him who made it for him he always answers with a laugh: 'That blacksmith is a genius, he made only this one and then he died struck down by divine wrath.'

'I'm happy you're here,' he tells me, 'but I'm not happy with the look on your face since you arrived.'

'It's true, it isn't cheerful, I'm very tired.'

'I thought that this evening we might organize a little party for our friends, invite a local group, light a big fire and dance as much as we want in the middle of the *battha*, Chinguetti's river of sand.'

'"That's a good idea but don't count me in.'

'Why not?'

'I already told you, I'm very tired.'

'Yes, but between now and then you will have rested.'

'No, I'm not going.'

'My friend, you're keeping something from me.'

I couldn't respond. He was getting on my nerves, I wanted to be alone. We were silent for a moment, I don't know why. I smell like tragedy, I suddenly thought. I carry the stench of death, it can be smelled.

'Fine, we'll party tomorrow in Ouadane.'

I said nothing. I wanted him to be quiet.

'The children love you,' he suddenly started again to break the heavy silence.

'Me too, I really like these kids.'

'All they do is talk about you and the marvelous story you told them, but I realize you want to be alone, you'll join us when you're in a better mood.'

'Marvelous stories', yes, the wonder is in the eyes, it's a cavity carefully implanted in us that waits to be filled with a story. I used to love stories when I was a child, I relished them, I told them to myself all the time, I used to live the tales, I breathed them, that thirst for the marvelous kept me company for a long time, a frenetic pursuit of the fantastic, a race toward the absolute that still makes me breathless.

Perhaps that was my downfall, the pursuit of nothingness, running after what I do not know. I should probably have been content with what life has to offer me. Yes, when I think about it, I'm nothing but a poor idler, weeping over a past that isn't his and not knowing how to look at what's around him. Because there it is, am I more unhappy than the wretches who don't even have a roof over their head, whose stomach is empty, the crippled beggars who clutter up our cities, the sick who can't seek any treatment, the shabby folks struggling in our streets, the convicts who rot away in prison? After all, I am a human being, which is a privilege as well, I'm not that dog I see sniffing the ground to survive, I'm not a cockroach, not a sheep being slaughtered, in short it's undoubtedly foolish to even say it, but it's an incredible bit of luck to be human, there are millions of billions of insects, birds, plants, forms of mildew who surely aren't aware of themselves, who don't say 'I'; while I think, I laugh, I speak, I love, I hate, I should be thanking God and not lamenting a fate that billions of species may be envious of.

What will become of me? I certainly won't have a future anymore, my future will be a prison cell, living eternally between four walls, with lice, hunger, criminals next to me, no, I'd rather die, no, if they sentence me to such abominations for the rest of my life I'll commit suicide, but no, I won't kill myself, I will resist, five, ten, twenty years, I'm bound to get my freedom back one day. I know Memed's story by heart, he murdered a man who had raped his sister, he spent ten years in prison and then picked up life where he'd left off, he married the woman who'd been waiting for him and then... But it isn't the same, he didn't already have a murderer-father, and there was honor, I don't even have a sense of honor, that madness that makes you do mad things.

I already see myself lying in the back of a dirty cell, my gaze turned gray for seeing nothing but four faded walls, my ragged nauseating face lined with misery. What would I be thinking about then? Which moments of my life would I be replaying to forget the deadening hours?

Time with Fati, for sure, and that night in the middle of the void in front of a shepherd's tent, he had put down a mat for us and a pillow, which was all the furniture he possessed, he'd brought us a teapot, small glasses, a brazier, and Fati sitting cross-legged began to prepare the tea, the shepherd had gone off to milk his animals, I was on my back humming to myself, the world had fallen silent, there was only the two of us and the sky.

No, I must erase Fati from my thoughts, I must not call her name anymore, or her lips, or the moments we spent together, I must cling to other memories, to a bliss from which she is absent, is there such a thing? Yes, absolutely, Tyarett for example.

That year I had refused to go to the Canary Islands with

my family, because my parents would sleep all day and spend all night in a casino playing Bingo, they'd leave me alone all the time, just a nice word every now and then, 'so, do you like it?', I'd walk along an overcrowded beach, I'd try to talk to gorgeous girls who would laugh at my accent, I'd eat enormous hamburgers and I'd come back with bitterness in my heart, the feeling of having missed out on an unimaginable world, a lighter complexion, and with a few extra pounds. I'd drink some fine beer without having to hide, and I'd gargle well before going back to the hotel, for although my parents weren't very religious they abstained as true nomads do, they abhorred alcohol, in their eyes the sole symbol of the city, therefore of the loss of indigenous culture. Yes, the people who are so tightly squeezed in today's narrow streets sometimes think of themselves as Bedouins, who knows why.

In Tyarett, where they had allowed me to go with Kader and a few other friends of mine, I had some unforgettable moments. During the day we'd protect ourselves from the scorching heat in well-ventilated straw huts or in the shade of leafy date palms, we'd tell each other a thousand jokes, romp about on the edge of the well, play *dhama*, the Bedouin checkerboard where the checkers are camel droppings and little acacia sticks. At night, we'd wear our finest clothes and would go wooing young girls whom we'd often frighten with our thriving city dwellers' faces. We would attend weddings to which we'd not been invited and where we'd dance to our heart's content and stay very late with the bride's friends. The sounds of the *ârdin and the tidinît*, our local harp and small guitar, sometimes drew us to the magnificent palm groves where we'd find a group of music lovers around a musician who was singing old tunes, every now and then repeating sweet quatrains that the guests had made up. At these gatherings we were quiet, delighted and intimidated by these men and women who were far less well-off than we, but whose calm joy of living, culture, or art of creating lovely words we didn't possess. We gorged ourselves on fresh dates, lamb's meat, and oblivion.

Are there other memories I would dwell on in prison, Fati again and her gentle charms, the time with the children last night? But probably even that string of faded images would only cause me pain.

Besides, would I even have time to replay all of this before my eyes? Maybe they'll sentence me to death, yes, that's possible, it's true they don't execute sentences like these any longer but for the son of the Cheikh's killer, an assassin himself, you never know. A friend of my mother's told me that a few years ago he had attended the last public execution. 'I don't know why I went there,' he said to me, 'perhaps because the city was empty, all of its inhabitants off to the beach to witness the execution. There were a lot of people, like a carnival, young girls carefully decked out, laughing eyes, sharp looks, peanut and tea vendors, as well as bearded men reciting sacred verses out loud. I noticed the condemned man from afar, he was in the prime of life, his eyes desperately calling for mercy. What? Exactly nothing, people turned away from him, he had killed the husband of his mistress, the people and the law rejected him, and I also noticed the 'commander of the blood', the victim's son who with a single word could change this capital punishment to life in prison. He raised his head in a gesture of defiance, a challenge to his own humanity because he said no, he refused to forgive, to spare the blood of his father's assassin; the judges, the religious scholars had pleaded with him, they had offered him huge sums of money but he said "no, he must pay, he must die, I want his blood", that was his right they explained to me, but I found it an appalling right. In the end they tied the poor fellow's body to a post and I closed my eyes before I heard the repeated salvos and the shouting of the crowd.'

My father was condemned to twenty years imprisonment, but for him that was a death sentence because he couldn't endure being in prison, and because he never stopped asserting his innocence. But was he actually innocent?

Why didn't I ever confide in anyone, why didn't I ever tell

my sad tale to anyone, which they say brings relief, but there's a distance between me and others that nobody has ever crossed, not even Mama, I planted trees inside myself, an entire shuddering forest that I won't let anybody come close to. Freudian complexes? Those are words that I read in books and that sometimes come to my lips spontaneously while in reality they're just wrong. No, they know nothing, those shrinks, I'd like to kill them all, they have the nerve to think that they know what sleeps deep down in our hearts, and what's that all about?

In fact, no one could know what lay inside me, I had buried it very deeply, like the djinn's treasure concealed beyond the seven seas, in an ocean of oblivion, at the very bottom, in a solid strongbox that contained another that contained another until the seventh one that was itself protected by seven solid metal bands.

I had learned to hide, to speak seven languages, I spoke to my mother one way, to my adoptive father in a different way, used another tone for my friends, hiding something from each one of them, a part of me that should not become visible. I really wasn't lying to anyone but I would disappear behind a screen of forgetfulness, yes, I'd clear my conscience of everything that at that moment needed to be expunged. I lived beneath the shadow of words and gradually developed a language purified of every word that was hurtful, I never spoke the word 'father' anymore, or 'family', God or Cheikh, crime or shame, or impiety, or anything that might stir up the burning feelings inside me that I was trying to obliterate. I didn't always manage it, and the very effort toward oblivion, deletion, sometimes grew even more painful, carrying more bitterness than the mere evocation of the words that hurt. True, I was lying to myself all the time. I was creating a fictitious world in which I wasn't myself, in which I was someone else, someone who wasn't carrying a load on his back.

But the whole wide world is nothing but lies. Everything we are we owe to mendacity, myths are invented for us, homelands are invented for us, as are ideologies and religions so that we'll play the role for which others have destined us.

I think I'm rambling a little. In the distance Chinguetti's minaret taunts the desolate landscape. I see it drift above the dark outline of the small clay houses. It isn't dead this minaret, it's fallen down more than once, they say, but quickly rose up again, it stayed upright for seven hundred years in the middle of sands, wars, famines. Why is it that some stones manage to resist time and others buckle under the first gusts of wind although they're made of the same materials, the same fears and anxieties? Time has such quirks! It sanctions some things and destroys others just as fast. And we start loving old ruins because we ourselves dream of continuing. It's those vestiges that delude us because they become embedded in our head and make us believe in eternity. For me time is the enemy, it is what created the Cheikh, condemned my father, and makes an assassin of me.

No, I am no assassin, I hadn't planned to kill her at all, had arranged nothing, it was mere chance and something hidden that screamed inside me.

It's too easy to put it that way but it may be true.

So let there be a civil war, terrible battles, so that everything that is silent will speak loudly, yes, have a reliable canon make centuries of silence and arrogance surrender. And then, too, it's certain that if there were an armed conflict my crime would be drowned under the weight of the atrocities, wars let everything else, even murders, be forgotten. Neither I nor the Cheikh's daughter will be the talk of the town anymore, only numbers will matter, two hundred today, eighty yesterday, dozens tomorrow and after a certain amount of time they'll do the count, so many thousands dead and vanished, so many cities ravaged, so much land laid to waste, so many lights extinguished. They won't enter the sufferings of the hearts in any records. The assassins of every day, the victims of every moment will be passed over in silence and, to ease their conscience, perhaps the arms sellers will try a handful of people for 'crimes against humanity'.

I see some children coming. They don't have bulging bellies or little navels that protrude from patched shirts, they're playing with old tires and somewhat oddly wander around this strange camp set up on a wild bit of land where there's no water at all.

The boldest of them makes a vague timid motion with his hand, I respond, and he has the courage to come closer.

'Hello.'

'Hello,' I say.

'Is it true, mister, that you give candy to children?'

I look around. Sidi sometimes brings sweets that he hands out on his way, especially to young girls. I don't see anything.

'Not now. Maybe later.'

'Is it true that your friends have huge cars that nothing can stop, not even the largest dunes?'

'No, that's the big rally, which doesn't come this way anymore.'

'Why not?'

'Because of the terrorists, I think.'

'Terrorists, are they bandits?'

'Yes, kind of.'

'Is it true that your friends buy everything and pay in dollars?'

'No, they only buy what they like and they don't pay in dollars.'

'Is it true that they give work to people?'

'No, why? You want to work, do you?'

'It's for his father,' another child intervenes, 'he has never worked in his life.'

He hasn't even finished his sentence when my little talker is already jumping on him, their friends clapping their hands to egg them on, I have trouble separating the two fighters.

The children gone, I try to pass the hours by reading a novel some tourist left behind, but the words refuse to enter my mind, the letters are hieroglyphs delineating my anxiety, the sentences can't cut through the fog in my brain, and Raya appears before me, eyes open, terrified, her image clings to me, torments me excruciatingly, I close my eyes and she is clearly displayed, nothing gets away, the gray sky, the timid waves, the bluish dress, the bare throat, the strands of hair falling down, the smile that disappears before a cry muffled by my hands. My entire body is shaking and tears flood my half-closed eyes once again. 'I've killed her,' I tirelessly repeat. I get up and leave the tent. The sun has settled right above my head, burning a land already consumed by its flames, the city appears like a mirage, the first houses resembling slumbering cages. In the distance a pick-up is approaching, breaking the silence, the noise of the motor offending drowsy ears. It's straining under enormous bundles on top of which sit unruffled, turbaned passengers.

A slight mist floats over the town from which no sound is heard. Yes, Chinguetti, I say to myself, has been asleep for a very long time. Since it's lost its prestigious image, it's closed its eyes, no longer wanting to see anything else. It breathes to the beat of time obliterated. Unexpectedly I dream of being there, of living forever in the middle of that city that has been dead for so long without knowing it. I imagine a life there, only there. I would live in a house made of clay, I would own a palm grove in Tendaoua'li, the neighboring oasis I know, take care of my palm trees and cultivate a tired field, every day I'd take sheaves of alfalfa, mint or dates and sell them at the market in town, I'd pray at the mosque five times a day, after prayers sit in the heavy shade of a wall to speak of trivial things always with the same friends, of the city's children who left not to come back, of the dried up well, of the rain that fell over there but ungratefully forgot about us, of the donkey of so-and-so who collapsed under too heavy a load, and of the few girls who want to go to the big cities and let their hair be visible. I would grow old serenely, without anguish because without a future, because everything is mapped out, nothing would happen to me anymore because nothing happens here, I would marry an ignorant and submissive country girl, I'd have children who would leave me as adolescents, their mother might follow them and I would die alone, buried in a grave that would already bear my name.

Fortunately, I tell myself, I have no children, the assassination saga will stop with me, no one will suffer because of me.

Am I myself not the son of nothingness? My sire has been expunged from the list of humans. The only one I found to defend him was Bouna, who was his friend, and who'd been in jail many times, for forgery and use of false papers, currency trafficking, alcohol trafficking, Bouna, not exactly a model of virtue. But why wouldn't they believe a man like him?

One day the hunger to know took me to this friend of my father's. I found him all by himself in the courtyard of his house. His torso was bare, he was wearing faded pants, and had eyes whose light was threatening to go out. He was stretched out on a mat, his head on two pillows, a radio crackling beside him, and a cigarette in his mouth. He didn't look up when I greeted him. Without a word he motioned for me to sit down. We stayed like that for a few minutes without speaking, then he said:

'Did you come about your father?'

I let out a quiet groan. I hadn't introduced myself yet.

'Well yes, I recognized you. You look like him. You're a man now, time must have gone by.'

'I've come to find out,'

'Find out what?'

'My father.'

'Your father was a man, a real man.'

'What does that mean?'

'That means that he loved life and knew how to face it, too.'

'Why did he leave the Cheikh to die in the desert? Why did he run away?'

'Ah, you believe their nonsense? They're liars, I tell you! Your father didn't do that, he would never do that. Despite the evil tongues, your father was a man of honor. Listen carefully, I'll tell you what happened.

Your father had just come to the end of some hard days as a guide for some fabulously wealthy emirs from the Gulf who'd come to the Dhar region with their big falcons to hunt gazelles and bustards. Now they no longer come because they've already massacred everything. They would always leave masses of slaughtered animals behind, which they killed only because they felt like it. Your father had earned a lot of money and wanted to relax for a few days in a camp located right next to Néma, the big city in the region. Your father would always stop en route when a heart called out to him, he loved life, may God forgive him.

The Cheikh wanted to get to a remote well in the middle of the Sahara where he'd arranged to meet some of his faithful followers. He came to Néma where they told him about your father and went to speak with him. But at first your father made his excuses: he'd only been to the well in question once, didn't know the area very well, the early summer was promising to be very hot and the period was apt to have sandstorms. The Cheikh insisted and promised a big reward. Your father was obliged to accept because of the money, yes, but most of all because one didn't turn down serious offers from the Cheikh. Still, moved by I don't know what instinct, he dragged his feet until the next day, but the Cheikh and his friends pressured him again. He couldn't get around it anymore. The Cheikh was accompanied by one of his disciples and a driver. The car, a Land Rover, was apparently in good enough condition. It had a barrel of diesel, a twenty-five liter jerrycan of water, and a case of mineral water in the back. At first your father balked at this: 'Why not bring more water?' 'That would weigh us down and, besides, with a good quantity of diesel we can get to the nearest water spot or go back to town if we want.' That logic didn't please your father who nodded skeptically. 'From that moment on,' he would later tell me, 'I felt things might take a bad turn, they seemed so confident, and for those who know the desert confidence like that is dangerous in itself, it's reckless; the only thing that can save those who wander these arid lands is foresight and wariness. But what could I do? It was the Cheikh, I had already resisted enough and as you know one doesn't ever refuse the Cheikh anything...'

So they left very early in the morning, it was still cold at the start of summer, that chill at dawn that often heralds a rough day. Your father showed the way, a point in the sky. He advised the driver not to move away from it, to skirt certain dunes that were too tough, but to always come back in the same direction. It was around ten o'clock that the wind rose, a terrible wind, sky and earth merged into a bitter vortex, they couldn't see anything anymore, the car bounced along above invisible mounds, they stopped for several hours waiting for calmer weather but the wind refused to be muzzled. That's when the Cheikh decided to get back on the road. Your father opposed it, he recommended that they wait a few more hours and then go back, even if it meant leaving the following day when the fury of the sky might have eased, but the Cheikh replied that he couldn't let his faithful wait any longer, who'd been assembled at the well since morning. "I knew right away," your father told me, "that we would get irrevocably lost because men like these believed only in their machine and didn't know that the desert doesn't put up with obstinacy or arrogance." They were moving ahead on the same path so they thought, but your father became more and more troubled, the wind was determined not to die down, the jolts of the car made them shudder from time to time, spirits were growing uneasy, and at a given moment the car itself showed signs of overheating. They stopped to give the motor a rest, the wind was gradually abating but the sun was still pouring out a thousand fires over an already blazing land. That's when your father looked around, leaned down to the rough ground, scrutinized the dunes outlined before them. "I don't know this place," he cried out, "I don't know where we are, I don't know which direction we should take anymore." Panic began to overpower their minds, the Cheikh's companion had tears in his eyes, the driver was swinging his arms and protesting in a foreign language, the Cheikh seemed to be meditating. The wait didn't last long, for the Cheikh gave the order to keep going in the same direction and the car moved off again. But they quickly sensed that the cooling system was beginning to fail, the red warning light was on for a few minutes more. They stopped and the driver went over to the water can to fill the radiator. That's when your father vehemently intervened, "No, water is now more precious than all the world's motors put together and even if it starts up again it won't do us any good because it may well stop again a little later. What we need to do is conserve the water and wait for help. Your faithful," he said to the Cheikh, "will surely begin to worry about your much too long delay and they'll come looking for us." The Cheikh didn't seem overly convinced. The driver mumbled a few vague words then raised the hood and poured a solid glassful of water into the motor, which began to purr and they got back on the road. No one said a word. Worry showed on their faces. They bumped along for almost an hour over soil that had become more sandy, the wind had picked up again, visibility was still limited, their hearts were pounding, all they could hear were the Cheikh's low chants, and from time to time a 'shit!' from the resentful driver. Every time the red light came on he'd stop and pour out some more water. Your father would protest just for form, since it seemed that no one heard him, the driver did what he wanted and the two other passengers now trusted only him. Your father crossed his arms and waited for an answer from heaven, because, he told me, "I was listening to the motor, I knew it was going to fail us, and I knew that not one of my companions would have the strength to brave the desert." After a languorous groan the motor finally stalled between two dunes and refused to comply with the driver's anguished cursing. The Cheikh sat down and began to pray, the driver was weeping, the Cheikh's disciple already had his eye on the water can and the few remaining bottles. Then, used to dangerous situations, your father made them a proposal: "Look, we're absolutely stuck. We have only very little water left but we must try to get out of this, the only imaginable door to salvation is that I go find help, the Sahara is big but it isn't empty, with a bit of luck I may find a camel driver, perhaps I'll come across a camp or a well, I'll be able to alert the authorities who'll come to your aid, they will use every means to find the Cheikh, they'll send well-made cars with experienced drivers and even an airplane. It's the only solution." They looked at each other, then nodded in agreement. But your father insisted that he take half of the remaining water with him. "I will be facing sun, sand and wind and I need to have enough water with me." After much discussion, they let him drink a glass of water and take two bottles along with him, a liter and a half in all. That left four bottles of mineral water and six liters in the jerrycan.

I'll spare you,' Bouna said to me, 'the horrors he lived through, the main thing is that he went north-west and never strayed from his path; the two bottles of water were quickly finished, he was sweating profusely and that way lost all his liquid, he thought he would die at any moment, he dug a hole where he burrowed down at night, and walked until he was exhausted, stopped, then had trouble getting up again, and soon he felt nothing anymore so he just kept walking, unaware of anything around him, staggering really, then miraculously on the fourth day he could make out some hoof prints, "Are they coming back to camp or are they going out to pasture?", he followed their trail and suddenly heard some children cry out: "A madman! A madman!", which is when he lost consciousness. When he opened his eyes again, he was lying on his back, a woman was washing his face with milk she was squeezing from her breasts, a man was pouring cool water over his whole body. He couldn't utter a word until the next day, which is when he alerted them to the fate of his companions, so a camel driver left immediately to notify the closest national guardhouse. Several cars went looking for them and found them the following morning, dead of thirst, the disciple and the driver intertwined, no one knew why. The Cheikh's face was turned toward Mecca, he'd written a few words on a piece of paper: "The guide has abandoned us, we don't know where we are, we are desperately thirsty." So they accused your father of having robbed them of their water, letting them die in the middle of the desert, the words he'd spoken to the nomads who had saved him were now used against him: "There was actually not enough water anymore for four. There was in fact no more than for one person, if that..." The Cheikh's disciples roused the entire country, they had powerful connections in the administration and the press, public opinion followed... Your father didn't have a chance.'

The children interrupted my thoughts. Nathalie snuggled up against me and touched my chin: 'So tell us the story...'. I tried to recall the beginning of the story I had started.

'Where were we?' I asked.

'Omom the good djinn, he wanted to go to Earth.'

*'Yes, Omom was moping a little. Still, he'd seen everything, he'd strolled on the most beautiful planets, he had fun amid the immense colors of the sun, he'd walked on Jupiter's rings, he'd spent a long time visiting Saturn and its satellites, he had set foot on the moon long before the Americans, but he really wanted to go to Earth.*

*His departure for Earth was tightly controlled by the Heart of the good djinns, for they felt that this planet was too dangerous because of the bad pollution and the hole it had dug in the* ozone, the covering that protects the Earth from the sun's rays; fake clouds were already shrouding it, carriers of a thousand dirty blots, and besides the bad djinns had conquered it a very long time ago, they'd put emperors in place to rule there, kings, dictators, and even regularly elected presidents, for that was another detestable feature of the Earthlings—they would entrust everything to people whom they would sometimes choose or who would often impose themselves, and these individuals had faces, words, human culture but, in reality, they belonged to the bad djinns who had inhabited them since their early youth and had primed them to govern their peers.

The Earthlings were the only ones in the whole universe who knew how to lie, they were the only ones in the whole universe who could be traitors, they were the only ones in the whole universe who were able to kill, for the bad djinns had conquered their spirits. So the Heart was beating very fast when Omom adamantly declared that he wanted to go to Earth. The mission to dissuade him was delegated to the oldest of the good djinns. He listened to him for a long time and then was quiet, he knew that his words would serve no purpose and that Omom was in the grip of an unusual frenzy known as passion, which doesn't listen to reason and cannot be defeated except by experience or age. He reported to the Heart: nothing could keep Omom anymore from attempting this strange adventure.

Thereupon the Heart's messenger gave him a mission: he was to carefully observe the Earthlings, acquire more knowledge than was offered by the countless documents the good djinns had amassed, and in particular he had to clearly determine the influence and the power of the bad djinns so that perhaps one day the Earth could get rid of them. That part of the mission had to be done with great delicacy, with great tact and caution, for the Heart didn't want to see the rebirth of the cosmic war that had broken out thousands of years ago between the good and the bad djinns, lasting for hundreds of years and ended with the demarcation of the territory and the zone of influence of each."

'Star Wars,' Evelyne called out. 'Tell us about that!'

'Another time, another time, now it's Omom we're interested in and his expedition to our planet.'

The other children agreed with me and I continued:

*'The Heart's messenger handed Omom an amazing machine, a kind of shimmering stone with bluish reflections.*

*"You will hide this carefully underneath the clothes you'll be wearing, all you have to do is touch it for it to respond to your wishes, you'll then know how to speak and understand every language on Earth, in the wink of an eye you'll be able to leave one place for another, you'll be able to disappear and appear before the eyes of the Earthlings, you'll be able to read what they write as well as their thoughts, above all you'll be able to distinguish between free men and those who are inhabited by the bad djinns.*

*The Heart wants you to come back before the moon reappears on the soil of the Sahara, for that's where you'll first land. Don't be late, or else the machine will break down and no longer function.*

*'So then I'd be staying on Earth?' Omom said, since he was worried that he might never get back to his own planet.*

*'Yes, you would become an Earthling, you would never be able to come back to us again, never. The machine wouldn't be worth anything anymore, except for its weight in diamonds, which for the poor Earthlings is not negligible.'*

*So Omom promised to respect the Heart's recommendations to the letter and was inwardly very moved at the prospect of at last making contact with the strange inhabitants of that very strange planet.*

*Omom put on the face, the clothes, and the unhealthy look of the Earthlings and flew off toward our planet. He was in a hurry. He didn't dawdle on his way, he didn't talk to the stars who were looking to have a chat, nor to the lazy clouds who invited him to have a glass of rain, nor to the rays of the sun who wanted to dance with him, nor to the awful winds who were laughing* stupidly, he was in a hurry to reach that rock lost in the middle of the oceans where people lived whose hearts had to a large extent been gnawed on by the foul fangs of the bad djinns.

He landed on a dune in the middle of the Sahara, not far from here I believe, yes, not far from here, at the edge of the Tiris region, where the sluggish grasses grow only during good years but dress in colors of green for several months. Omom looked around and saw nothing, he wondered what had become of the humans, nature in her nakedness remained mute, although the sky was adorned in all its flames. Through the glistening stars he caught sight of the faint light of his distant homeland and suppressed a vague feeling of homesickness that was already trying to seep into him, "no, tomorrow, later..."

He walked for a long time, alone in the desert, didn't meet one living soul, the entire earth was silent, no fox appeared, no bush stood in his way, no voice could be heard, silence shouted the solitude of the world. Yet Omom knew very well that this planet was the noisiest one in the whole universe, he knew that it dumped billions of decibels into the vast space, that the majority of its inhabitants no longer discerned the sounds that at every instant damaged their hearing as well as their understanding. The bad djinns would clog up their ears to steal their spirit.

Again Omom walked for a long time, of course he wasn't afraid of anything because djinns don't know fear, he didn't feel any fatigue or hunger because djinns do not know fatigue or hunger, but he was eager to meet humans, to speak with them, see them live and bustle about, and also to understand why such fragile beings managed to construct such enormous things and do so much harm to those around them.

Suddenly, as he was sliding down a large dune, he heard singing. It was a crystalline voice, not strong but filling the sky, it ran right through Omom's body and he felt a movement he had never known before, a tremor of his whole being, as if a sweet and fragrant draft was passing through him. For the first time he started his machine to be one with time, the minuscule device *that the Heart had entrusted to him when he had taken on the Earthling body. The device crackled at first, then a voice finally reached him, very clear this time:*

He has left my Beloved
In a machine from heaven
But he will come back one day
And I shall be so beautiful

*Omom came closer and saw a young girl holding a bucket on her head with both hands, bobbing under its weight. Her body was already half wet, showing outlines of her shape, he said to himself immediately, drawn by a fine artist's hand. She didn't seem concerned about it. She was humming a dreamy tune, swaying to the flow of her voice.*

*Omom approached very slowly and voiced a greeting he intended to be respectful.*

*The girl jumped and at first Omom had trouble understanding her cries.*

*His time machine crackled a little, then at last he heard: 'My God, a djinn!' The water spilled out.*

*'Don't be afraid,' he said to her, 'I'm just passing through so I'll give you a hand.'*

*'Ah, I thought you were a djinn.'*

*'Oh really! And why wouldn't I be?' he said laughing.*

*'Djinns have very long noses, enormous mouths, they don't have a body, just vapor, no, I know, you're not a djinn, you actually look very nice, but you did scare me,' she said, 'and now I have go back to the watering hole again.'*

*'That's no problem,' he said to her, 'I will go and fill your bucket.'*

*'I'll wait here for you,'*

She showed him the way and he found a small muddy area where two emaciated camels were already drinking. Omom leaned down and in a single motion filled the bucket.

When he came back he found her sitting on the top of a dune from where you could see the tents of the camp, lost in a foggy twilight.

'You look tired,' she said. 'Maybe you'd like to rest a bit?'

Omom sat down beside her, he didn't say a word. He, the good djinn so superior to the Earthlings, was intimidated by this young girl who'd emerged from the heart of the sands, who had no power and who knew nothing. Her hair in braids that covered half her face, which she'd constantly lift, the little pucker of her lips, the frown on her forehead, and her laughing eyes busy reading the indistinct lines traced on the sand, all this caused unfamiliar movements to stir inside him. She was completely absorbed in her task. Her slender nimble fingers were meandering across the fine sand. Every now and then she whispered some inaudible words, smiling a little, and would then go back to her hieroglyphs, indecipherable even to him. Omom was watching her, both in surprise and admiration. He told himself that it was a miracle to meet a pure soul right after arriving on Earth, a soul that hadn't been devoured by the bad djinns, for the Heart had cautioned him: the Earthlings who are the captives of bad djinns couldn't smile at good djinns nor accept their company. They were surrounded by a thousand invisible rings that blocked their eyes, ears, and spirits. It was the way the bad djinns guarded their prey. This young girl was free and she didn't know it.

She pointed at the signs she had formed.

'Do you know how to decipher that?' she asked him

He had to admit his ignorance, the Heart hadn't taught him everything.

'Those are words of the sand and the winds, they are aimed at humans to tell them the future, but not everyone understands this language, only very knowledgeable women, like my mother.'

'How can you not understand signs that you yourself have traced in the sand?'

'Ah, you trace them without knowing, without thinking, you let your fingers gently walk across the sand, that's all, of course you have to respect the forms, but at first they don't speak to us, it's when you look at them that the future begins to emerge.'

'And what about you, do you know how to make the sand speak, even just a little?'

'Yes, a little, I've only learned a very little bit, you see that line and those two dots that cap it, I think those are two hearts joining, brought by the good path of destiny, but more than that I do not know.'

'I know,' Omom said.

'You know?'

'Yes, they are on powerful ships that come from two planets very distant from each other, they will confront roaring winds, ferocious seas, they will go through thousands of torments but they will meet each other in the middle of a desert where only lovely hearts grow.'

'That's beautiful what you just said,' she whispered as she turned to him. 'Tell me more!'

'I will tell you that over there where I come from, I heard a voice that told me: "Go now, you have an appointment with a smile".'

'And am I that smile, tell me, am I that smile?'

'Yes, maybe so.'

'No, not "maybe", it's certain, truer than the sun that is now getting ready to go to sleep, it's true, and I felt it when I saw you, you are the unknown steed who will take me to undreamed of shores.'

'Shores?'

'Yes, a new continent, very far away, so close perhaps.'

*Then as Omom held out his hand and the young girl didn't pull hers away, he noticed a new and intense flow go through his body.*

*She stood up, dusted off her clothes and said:*

*'I'm already late, my parents will start worrying about me, I have to get back to the camp.'*

*'Me too, I still have far to go, see the world, I will come back here.'*

*'I will wait for you,' she said to him with an unwavering look.*

All the way on the top of a big mountain the ruins of Ouadane raise their head. You can see them from afar. Their brown mass draws a dust-covered painting beneath the sky.

In the valley the palm trees form a bundle of greenery trembling under the threat of the white sand and the stony plain. They're vainly striving to attract inevitably magnetized glances toward the rocky summits. It's true that, like Chinguetti, Ouadane really has nothing going for it but its past. A passive, sleepy city that seems to have abandoned any thought of showing up. Still, it's not bad to live among these clay houses and the dust-covered streets. I lived there for a few days in the winter, all you heard was the blowing of the wind or the muezzin's voice, many of the inhabitants had left the wadi right after the last dates were picked, and those who'd stayed were hiding, silent. The people of Ouadane have always spoken softly and observed from afar, they've always mistrusted the unknown, they've watched for dangers from the top of the ramparts they erected to keep the monsters away. They've been robbed throughout history, for they were too hardworking in the midst of indolence, too rich among the starving, too abstemious in the midst of excess, too pious in the midst of a sea of indifference, too thrifty as well, and too culti-vated. In each house of Ouadane there lay hidden a secret loft, the ultimate defense against looters, where they would hide wheat, dates, their women's virtue and fine manuscripts, gold coins and ostrich feathers, the city would become self-sufficient when it was besieged, for inside its walls it had its well, its enormous reserves, its marabouts who from the high ramparts would send talismans to blind the invaders, deprive them of water and food, disrupt their minds, wither the bellies of their wives, and make them go away forever.

The journey has been long and I'm exhausted. We choose an inn at the foot of the mountain. Zayda, the boss, knows how to talk to foreigners, she knows how to smile, too, the service shouldn't be bad, I stretch out inside a tent and close my eyes, the children are crying out as they spread their hands toward the tall ruins as Zayda introduces the city to her guests in her rough voice, a donkey brays in the distance. The atmosphere is full of sounds that can't be identified, I cannot sleep, the trip was long and through my closed eyelids I see my mother. She's holding her head in her hands and she's weeping, I imagine her sufferings, her only son lost, accused of a crime, she who's never hurt anyone, here she is, a former wife and mother of murderers, she who has spent her whole life chasing the evil specter, here she is diving into it again, she who has forgotten it all, here are the old demons coming back to her.

Zayda brings us bowls filled with camel's milk, the tourists only have a tiny taste of it at the tip of their tongue, Sidi and I relish it.

Zayda, I know her, a woman who doesn't ask any questions, you can feel she's happy in this city at the end of the world, where she's created a universe that gravitates around her, an inn where she welcomes strangers, a community life that blends traditional games with charitable actions, a large family around her, and all of it started from nothing, a small business in fresh mint and necklaces, she built it all up from smiles and patience. It's true that she manages to stick to this little spot without really blending in, you can sense she's a stranger and at the same time she's comfortably settled, she talks to us about Ouadane as her thing, about the local culture, the season of the date harvest that's approaching, her tribe that has gone to the big cities, with a barely perceptible ounce of pride, but also with a certain sadness. Is she afraid of seeing this town of unstable stones vanish? It's astonishing how attached one can remain to stones!

And I, am I still attached to the casbah that saw me come into the world? It's when I, still very young, left Atar that the first questions rang out, that I heard my father's name whispered very quietly so that I wouldn't hear it, and then slip-ups that gradually made me question myself, and then the almost inevitable evocation of the tribe from which I come.

My mother wanted to cut the thread that links me to two phantoms she dreaded, Atar where she was born and the tribe of the man who had loved her there.

My mother was only willing to mention the name of my father's tribe to me one single time. She told me that nomads do not pronounce its name at night because it attracts armed bands, yes indeed, its mere evocation causes anxiety throughout the Sahara.

'It's true that the people of your tribe know no fear, and it's true that they are often fine poets, and it's true,' she added, 'that they even know how to be generous, but they are thieves,' she warned me, 'who know nothing about anything, who respect nothing, only themselves or the occasional tribes with whom they are associated, they're uncultivated and have no religion, they're lazy and ignorant and never do anything with their hands, in their eyes working is degenerate, in their eyes love is weakness, and God is merely an occult force to whom you must pray from time to time before you go out to rob His creatures. Just watch out! At times when they might try to approach you, walk away, as fast as you can!'

'Am I not one of them, Mama?'

'No, you are my son, it's Ahmed and I who have loved you and raised you, you have no connection with them.'

'So why are you telling me about them?'

'Because I know that one day they'll try to contact you, your aunt, too, must have praised their fake qualities to you.'

I did nothing to draw attention to Mama's contradictions when she said: 'it's Ahmed and I who've raised you', although she had initially left me in my grandmother's arms, she said 'your people' while she wanted them to become strangers to me, she said 'your father's tribe', while she added that my only parents were just her husband and herself.

The conversation turns to Guelb Er-Richât, a giant crater, one of the largest in the world, located at almost forty kilometers from here, the eye of humanity they pompously say. If it were up to me, I'd gouge out the eye of humanity so that it can no longer see me. With a look Sidi invites me to talk about it, I pretend not to understand because I'm not in the mood to go into raptures over a huge hole in the ground and furthermore it would oblige me to accompany them there. Then they start fantasizing about this lost meteor, glimpsed by a wandering soldier and the one that Théodore Monod searched for all his life. I fail to say that it was perhaps just a hallucination, a mirage of bare spaces, but Sidi's look calls me to order, I know what that means: 'You shouldn't kill the dreams of tourists, it's what they come for… and besides, you never know, this area has been explored so little, there behind those dunes we see, there may well be the most absolute desert in the world the Majabat al-Koubra, the Empty Quarter, you can imagine anything.'

But I imagine only the turmoil that would follow the discovery of Raya's body. Her face that seems so innocent will be plastered all over the social media. What virtues will they attribute to her? Her parents, her friends will attest to her qualities, the entire country will grieve over her, a young girl, so beautiful, so well born, the victim of a sadist, an ostentatious funeral, thousands of people will pray behind an imam with a broken voice. And me, what will they say on the day that fingers will point at me? His father's son, heir of bad genes, assassin of expectations, the perfect villain.

But why would I let myself fall into their hands? Maybe I should flee still farther, leave the country or even die before they capture me and sentence me once and for all to a slow and dishonorable end. Flee? Where to? The Sahara? I would die of thirst or become a prisoner of the dark Bedouins who would sell me to the authorities as a slave on the run. Kill myself? I won't have the courage and then, too, what would my death produce other than bereavement for my only Mama? In any case, I have killed, and that will pursue me forever, that will disturb me eternally, I will never again know peace. I might as well surrender right away and free my mind. Yes, tomorrow I will leave Sidi and his friends, I'll go down to the city and I'll tell the whole story.

But maybe they'll never find her? Her body might vanish forever. The tide will rise and carry her off into the depths of the ocean, they will look for her everywhere but no one will think of the sea, thousands of her father's fold will follow her traces, a thousand questions will be asked: was she kidnapped? Is she a hostage somewhere? Was she the victim of her father's sworn enemies the Salafists? The electronic sites, the newspapers will carry headlines: What happened to the Cheikh's daughter? The imams will pray for her from their high pulpits, the embarrassed government will command all their cops to find her dead or alive, and in the end, perhaps, a visionary will see her in his sleep and shout in the streets the next day: 'I dreamed of her, I dreamed of the saint's daughter, her blessed father has called her and she decided to join him, she is with him, in the beyond, enjoying the fruits of Eden!' Then in the minds of many she will be a saint and she will be invoked in countless prayers. Raya, a saint, the thought alone makes me laugh already. But no, it's loathsome to laugh when you have blood on your hands, and even if they don't find her, she will stay with me, she will torture me forever. Tomorrow I shall tell the whole story.

Fati tortured me in the end also, she made light of my

feelings, of my consideration for her, of my 'immaturity' as she said. She always kept me waiting a very long time. She had her meetings, her appointments, her readings, her thousand things to do and, at loose ends I could only patiently wait and pray that she would appear, that she would let me come into her arms for just a little while. I now think that in her eyes I'd come to be no more than an embarrassing thing she had to keep occupied, I did her shopping, I wrote her speeches, I answered her telephone. Ah yes, of course, my consolation lay in those happy moments that I would steal from her over-scheduled hours.

Why then did I become infatuated with her? One couldn't call her particularly pretty, her features were too regular, her face was wide, her legs too skinny... Legs are important for us, anyway it's true that she was pretty, but in the way that people often are, she had... I believe it was her eyes and her smile that delighted me, they were an invitation to an adventure, well there I go, just babbling, I loved her that's all, it was as absurd as it could be.


The old city of Ouadane. To reach it you have to climb a steep street built on the side of the mountain, which I scale at a run with the children and we make it to the top, out of breath. The others are struggling to join us. We go through the quiet alleys, cut stone houses, vending stalls that seem not to have had any customers for a long time, children who don't run after us or look at us as if we were Martians, and a woman who stops, covers her face and turns toward the wall to let us pass.

We encounter no one in the old city, the age-old alleyways now have names but only those of its ulemas. The street of the Forty Scholars. This is where the town's sages used to live. A student could intone his chants from the Koran as he was crossing town and it's said that there would always be an instructor on his route who would correct his mistakes. The only history they talk about here is of the scholars, the wars the city lived through, the famines, the long sieges, the emirs who sometimes imposed tithes that were too high, all of it now obliterated. Ouadane only wants to remember what made it shine, its stones, its books. We walk among the ruins, we stop under long walls weakened by time and every so often dangerously bowing their head, they're stooped with age for having stood there for centuries, we bend over the well that would be used when leaving town was too dangerous, the walls now restored. Without any discussion, the children and I are suddenly running down the steep cliff to reach the palm groves all the way below. The others are calling at us from afar but we pretend not to hear, we fly across the rocks, we laugh and shout very loudly, I feel a window opening inside me that lets an unexpected breath of gaiety pass through, we get there panting a little but happy. The wavering shadow of a tall palm tree greets us. The children are laughing wildly: 'We've left them behind, they're still up there!' Roger chortles as he dives laughing into my arms. I don't know what to do with this glee that's come over me all of a sudden.

Zayda has lit a huge fire right in front of the inn. There's a *degdaga* waiting for us, the mythical dance of the Ouadane people. Zayda has also pitched a spacious tent, with tapestries and cushions. One by one the men and women of the town arrive, the children following them. The *degdaga*, I'm told, is practiced less and less in Ouadane, it's too happy a dance and people no longer know how to smile, it's a wild dance and people no longer know how to let go, it's a vigorous dance and people no longer have the strength, it demands enthusiasm and the hearts have grown subdued.

Fati could really dance, dancing was her secret. We'd leave the city, come to the first dunes, she'd open her phone and gently sway to the rhythm of the *knou*, she loved that languid, silent style, the slow and melodious pace, the griot would gently play his tidinît and she'd shift from one foot to the other in the moonlight, arms forward, following the rhythm, her head high, proud, on the tip of her heels, the *knou* is the dance of princesses she liked to say. True enough, *knou* is the music that cradles desires and dreams, I immediately have a strong longing to hear it, but this is not the moment for impossible dreams.

I spoke with Moulay, I knew that he was one of the Cheikh's followers but I wanted to have their version, the one that the tribunal upheld. I introduced myself under a different name, as a student doing research on the life of the Cheikh.

He was fat, with shaggy hair, a protruding belly, a neatly cut beard, a brand new blue boubou, matching blue pants that came down to his knees, and a bare torso displaying large pectorals. He remained lying on his side, his right hand at his temple, displaying a look of oppressive fatigue.

'The Cheikh,' he told me, 'is a pole of his time, he combined knowledge and generosity...'

I had to interrupt him with great courtesy, even if some irritation crept into my voice, true, I simply couldn't tolerate the dithyrambs praising the Cheikh anymore, I took them as an insult, I couldn't listen to the pompous speech that was about to follow.

'No,' I said to him, 'I know all that, the only thing that interests me now are the circumstances of the Cheikh's death.'

'The Cheikh,' he said, 'had a premonition of his end, he knew that God had called him. He had to go to the well of Tanit where his faithful were waiting for him, he sensed that he wouldn't come back, but he couldn't be deaf to destiny's calls, he couldn't disappoint his talibés, his Koranic students. So he said farewell to his wives, his children, his faithful followers, and he left to follow the course that providence had laid out for him.

God put the devil on his path, who was to drag him to his death. He was a man of the Tekatt tribe, pillagers as everybody knows, a group of adventurers, but the best connoisseurs of the desert and its every corner. The Cheikh was accompanied by one of his closest disciples, Brahim, may God welcome him into His holy Paradise, and a Senegalese driver, Diop, also one of his faithful.

They left at dawn one holy Friday. It was definitely a windy day, the well was definitely far away, but that devilish murderer already had an elaborate plan in his head and the fury of the day's weather was in his favor. He wanted revenge. A few years prior, the Cheikh had taken sides in a conflict concerning the ownership of a well that pitted his tribe against another. The Cheikh had declared that the well should go to its original owners and that what had once been stolen by force should go back to its legitimate proprietors. The assassin's tribe protested vehemently but the government interceded to apply the fatwa.

So this evil man took advantage of the bad weather to disorient the Cheikh and his friends, then used the night's darkness to steal all their money, the little water they had left, and went away thereby condemning them to certain death.'

I'd never heard anything about this conflict that my father's tribe had been involved in. I only knew that it was hardly inclined to bring charges before a court that would always convict it. I also knew that it almost never takes things out on the marabouts whose talismans it feared.

Neither could my father have hatched a plan, for I'm absolutely certain that he really didn't want to accompany the Cheikh that day, but that he'd been forced to do it.

Finally, I also knew that the Cheikh and his companions had not had their water stolen because a jerrycan and empty bottles of mineral water had been found near their bodies. Not a word about that was said at the trial, but each one of them had kept more water than my father had taken with him when he went off all by himself to face the sandstorm and the fury of the sky. As for the money, none of it was found on my father.

I didn't tell my interlocutor any of this, he would have been offended and called me all kinds of evil names, perhaps he would even have rallied the Cheikh's followers against me and my identity would have been disclosed.

But what would all this matter today, what would my father's innocence do for me even if it were laid bare in broad daylight, even if he were proven innocent by all the world's courts, today it's about me, it's me, only me, who wears the cloak of infamy.

A classmate once invited us, my friend Bâ and me, to his house. His mother, a tall, beautiful woman, greeted us with a lovely smile. But when I was introduced to her, she asked what my mother's name was and then added: 'She doesn't have any children with her second husband so you must be Barhoum's son'. My father's name reverberated painfully in me and I even faltered a bit, I thought I saw a flash of disdain in the woman's eyes, I think I moved my shoulders as if to say, 'so what?' but it was only to hide the turmoil inside me. She said nothing else and went off to do her household chores. She even gave us a warm smile when we left. The scene stayed with me for a long time. She'd spoken my father's name with pursed lips, almost spelling it, with a reluctance that felt as if he carried a malevolent force inside him, and I received it like a cannonball, an assault on me. Why didn't I learn early on to discard the old complexes and carry the name, not proudly—that would have been impossible—but indifferently, the way you live with lips that are too thick or a neck that is too long?

The *degdaga* began while I was still wholly immersed in myself, I hadn't even seen them coming, the men in their wide boubous and belts and the women adorned as if for a grand party.

At the sound of the drum and the flute, the men jump into

the middle of the circle, whirling around the huge fire, uttering high-pitched cries, dancing on one foot, tossing rifles into the air and catching them with a rhythmic and fierce expression on their faces, the flaps of the boubous flying, while the women clap their hands and jiggle the long strings of beads that encircle their heads, singing about their 'very brave men' coming back from afar. Originally, the *degdaga* was often danced to actually welcome the arrival of the caravans, expressing joy, the end of isolation, the anxiety of famine now fading, and also the hope of encounters, reunions, new weddings, possible happiness. I'm well aware that this is a *degdaga* for tourists, the best dancers aren't here, for they were engulfed long ago by the illusions of big cities, Ouadane's blood was sucked by brighter lights, I know, these men here are just poor peasants who for a few pennies try to embrace the rhythms of days gone by, I know, but maybe it's with these dances that they'll find the rhythms and soul of those times, that they'll feel they're dressed in the old burnooses of the true traditions.

For a moment I forget the noises and descend into myself through the great inferno before me, the fire calls me and I dive back into it, I read my clearly charted hours there, I inscribe my grueling moments there, the tears I've let flow, and my mother's aggrieved face, I no longer hear the sounds of the *degdaga*, now it's Raya's face that stares at me and screams, her cries separating me from the embers, now I notice them distinctly, for I was deaf when I was squeezing her throat. Whom was she calling out to for help? Me or the distant presence of the solitary fisherman who couldn't hear her.


The children jumped all over me while I was still deep in my distress. They plopped down on the sand in front of me, chin on their hands. The *degdaga* had stopped and only the crackling of the wood was talking. The adults were sitting some distance away around the fire and were visible to us only in a pale light. I drew back into myself, closed my eyes a little then opened them again to refresh the lines of the story and the music of the words.

'*So Omom went off to conquer the Earth, fathom the secrets of this very desert-like, yet very swamped planet. Until now he had only touched upon the essence of things, the primary soul. For him the young Bedouin woman who had beguiled him so was like touching the naked truth of the Earthlings...*'

"Was she naked, the young Bedouin?' Evelyne asked.

'No, I simply mean that she was true, she wasn't covered in the thick varnish that the great civilizations, the great human constructions, use for dressing people.'

'I don't understand', Roger said.

Indeed, I had put a bit too much grown-up material in the story. I should disentangle myself.

'What I mean is that she was a simple girl, living in a more natural environment than we do.'

'Aren't we in nature then?'

'Well, yes, but our life is full, completely full of our own creations, well... it's too long to explain... and besides none of this is part of the story. Can I go on?'

The small heads nodded.

'*So Omom flew away to get to know the world. He drifted for a long time in the ether, watching everything on Earth pass by, he could clearly see the continents, the rivers, the lakes, the ice and fire deserts, the mountains, the forests and, drowned out by the cacophony, the cities where the majority of Earthlings have taken shelter. All of it seemed heartbreaking to him at first. Metal waste parts were floating through space, an immense cloud of black smoke was escaping from the cities and the Earthlings' endless chatter was already reaching his ears. 'What are they screaming about so loudly, you'd think they're squabbling, yes it's all about squabbling and about wars, too, I hear the noise of weapons, the bad djinns aren't lounging around.' A kind of weariness assailed him at the thought of having to confront these pathetic beings, enslaved by the bad djinns from now on. 'Should I go there?' he wondered. The image of the young Bedouin girl appeared before him, 'Shouldn't I go back to the land of sands, listen to her again, wander around amid unsteady predictions... Her choppy speech, her eyes lighting up, her crystalline laugh... Shouldn't I go back to the place the bad djinns have spurned? No,' he finally told himself. 'I'm no coward, I couldn't run away, what would they say about me on our planet over there? I have come to explore the cave, I can't stop at the entrance, I must brave this Earth where our enemies the bad djinns rule, understand how they could have secured such power, maybe shield the humans from their malevolent influence, after all I have a mission to complete.'*

*He dropped onto an avenue of a large metropolis. Of course he made no sound, no one turned around when he appeared, and he found himself quite naturally walking among the people. He realized that they were hardly looking at each other, they were walking on the same sidewalks but didn't mingle, they were together but each one was alone, face tense, withdrawn into themselves. It pained him a little, for he knew that the bad djinns created gigantic spaces between people, cultivating indifference, fear, contempt, and then hatred in them. An incessant din hovered above their heads, giant roars sprang out from everywhere, earsplitting rumbles burst from the sky, the Earth, and the four corners of space. Omom used his machine to diminish the racket in his ears, but he realized he was the only one worrying about it, apparently the people were hearing nothing, kept on wandering, completely unrattled by the noise, and those who were wearing helmets did so for an entirely different reason. Omom quickly grasped that the Earthlings were deaf and didn't know it.*

*He stopped in front of a department store, men and women were coming out with arms full of strange packages, he went in, a massive profusion of objects of all sorts greeted him, men stood in line to purchase new gadgets, new phones, food they could find in nature, drinks that didn't quench anyone's thirst, clothing that unclothed you, ineffective medications, dreams that didn't uplift anyone. Omom realized that all they were doing was buying, that this was their sole perspective, and that their hearts were beating faster over weird articles they truly didn't need at all.*

*Then, to his great surprise, he discovered that the Earthlings weren't speaking, they merely had thousands of images glued inside their brains and their retinas to which they attached sounds, words stripped of any profound significance to which they gave no thought at all and that came from their gullets not from their hearts or minds.*

*Omom roamed at great length through the cities of today, he went to all the grand metropolises, he saw the arrogance people carried within, the bad djinns had infused them with the conceit that caused them to forget life, they erected immense things like the mirrors where they sought their own reflections to glorify themselves, even wealth made no sense, for those who were rich had so much of it that they could only spend small bits of it, while the rest would flatter their ego, the poor remained poor not because they lacked for everything but because temptation created anguish and unfulfilled conquests in them. The affluent countries had surrounded themselves with citadels guarded by thousands of policemen, soldiers, functionaries, sailors. And outside the walls the real poor, the displaced, were begging for a right of passage and looking toward a West that was looking the other way. The well-heeled of poor countries sometimes had rights of passage and were, besides, highly useful: they helped to contain the flux of the wretched who would drown in the brackish waters that removed opulence, while they themselves were very opulent and obstinately strove to appear what they were not, they despised their cultures, they copied the ways, customs, and the drivel of the peoples who were free and rich.*

*Omom visited temples, churches, mosques, but faith no longer filled people's hearts, and those who strongly believed they had it would sometimes take the winding path of hollow certi-*

*tudes or the bloody one of hate-filled utopias.*

*Omom walked around for a long time without ever being able to talk to anyone, his machine that had been able to speak with the young Bedouin girl could not untangle the language of the cities, it would crackle painfully when he questioned it. For a moment he thought he was lost, his mission defeated, his glorious return compromised, but then he heard a child speak to his mother:*

*'Mama, I want happiness.'*

*And she bought him a toy.*

*'Mama, I want silence.'*

*And she bought him a little shrieking machine.*

*'Mama, I want the sky.'*

*And she bought him candy.*

*Omom understood that the earthly adults, whose souls had been invaded by the bad djinns, were forgetting the language of origins that only children still possessed.*

*He went over to the child and spoke to him:*

*'I want to be your friend.'*

*The child looked at him with delight and held out his hand, but the irate mother gave Omom a frightened look and dragged her son away.*

*Omom now knew that the bad djinns had corrupted the true language of humans forever and had subjugated them by imposing words on them that no longer conveyed their meaning.*

*He kept on walking among the Earthlings for a long time, he didn't approach them much anymore so that he wouldn't be recognized too soon by the bad djinns, he watched them graze wildly in life's meadows without a single look toward their own future. And that's when he noticed people in a large city gathered around a man who was speaking as he held his hands raised to the sky. He quietly moved closer and, unimaginably, understood what he was saying. It was a poet. Yes, poetry borrows from the stars and speaks the language of hearts, a sweet music accompanied it and it, too, was speaking. Omom went over to the poet and the musician, he waited a long time for the crowd to disperse so he could finally approach them, but then he saw them packing up their things and getting ready to leave. They were also counting the money they'd made and both were smiling, apparently very happy with their good fortune. Omom's heart cringed because he'd hoped that it was art alone that interested these artists and not the colored paper the bad djinns had created to imprison the Earthlings' heart. Nevertheless, he spoke to them anyway:*

*'It made me happy to hear you speak and sing in the language of the heart.'*

*Stunned, the two artists looked at each other.*

*'Yes,' Omom went on, 'art saves one from slavery, it liberates long-buried souls, you are free men because you know how to sing words and rhythms that are liberating.'*

*Pointing their finger at him the two men burst out laughing.*

*Then Omom knew that they didn't understand. They only knew how to sing uplifting words but they weren't climbing the mountains that lead to truth, their feet remained stuck in solid ground, held by heavy chains, they were sniffing the air of liberty from a distance, disseminating it to others who in turn raised their nose high to catch a whiff of the perfume of real things, but they remained deaf to the calls of their profound being. For centuries the bad djinns had all the latitude needed to shackle the Earthlings securely.*

*So Omom left, very upset, ashamed to have to go back to his city with empty hands, without having completed the mission the Heart had delegated to him.*

*He rushed into the old alleyways of a city in a poor country and walked around among crying miseries and dancing loves. He entered stinking bars and darkest dives, he rubbed shoulders* with drug dealers, prostitutes and beggars, with crowds that sing to God and those that foment revolutions.

And as he turned the corner of a desolate street he heard someone call to him, he searched a long time in the intertwining little streets of the poor town without knowing where the voice came from until he discovered a man sitting alone in the middle of a trash heap, laughing as he looked at Omom.

'I could see right away that you've come from far away, from a planet where they still know how to speak,' the man said.

'Who are you?' Omom asked, 'and how is it that together with the children you're the only one who still knows the Earthlings' true language?'

'It's because I'm crazy, my good friend.'

'Crazy, you who among millions of people are one of the few who still know how to speak?'

'Yes, you know this is where the bad djinns rule, their power is extraordinary.'

'But at least you aren't their slave.'

'Who told you I'm not?'

'You know how to speak, you're not blind, you're not deaf, and you have a heart.'

'That's true and that's why they've declared that I'm crazy, that I've lost all common sense and that they ought to tie me up or have me locked up or let me loiter around, adrift, without anyone listening to me, and the others wouldn't understand me anyway, they've lost the meaning of words.'

'I heard a poet and a  musician who could speak.'

'Yes, music and poetry have been acknowledged as the true language of humans, just to rest the souls for a tiny moment, because people occasionally do remember the language of the gods so, just so nostalgia doesn't become an awakening, they spray them with it from time to time. But once he's recited or written it, if he wants to continue to be accepted and not be shackled, the poet must immediately forget the language of real humans or else he'll be declared accursed; he will become "crazy" and they'll lock him up, some drown themselves in alcohol or religion, others kill themselves. In any case, anyone who doesn't adhere to the new order imposed by the djinns will be removed from society, "out", beyond the borders of sub-humanity.'

'Not all djinns are that way, just the bad djinns.'

'That's true, but they are the most powerful.'

Omom felt forced to agree.

'And what about the children, they do know how to speak, don't they?'

'Yes, but they're not aware of what they actually are, and they're quickly taught to erase everything, they have to undergo a heavy apprenticeship and if they don't succeed, if they don't manage to forget what they are, then they'll be rejected, they'll die or they'll become prisoners.'

'So you are a prisoner?'

'Yes, the most difficult of incarcerations, nobody listens to me, everyone's afraid of me, even the children though they still understand my language, they're dragged away, they're told that I'm dangerous, that I'm "crazy". Yet it's a good thing that this country isn't wealthy enough, or else they would have locked me up in a hospital with lots of nurses, lots of psychiatrists, to sentence me to permanent isolation.'

Omom stayed with him for a long time, they discussed all kinds of things, the "madman" needed to be heard because no one ever listened to him. Omom wanted to better understand this abysmal fall of the Earthlings and how the bad djinns had conquered their planet and their bodies and their hearts and the deepest of their thoughts. He recognized that the Earthlings were lost, that several more centuries might be needed before they would be able to pull themselves together and win back their liberty. He also knew that his mission had come to an end and that he had to return to his distant planet.'

What madness to want to go to Oualata, pass through deserts and cross rough terrain to a city that's not waiting for you, because I know that Oualata doesn't want to see anyone, hundreds of kilometers separate it from other people, and it likes to be left alone and admire itself in its mirror of sand, in the drawings on its walls and the illuminations of its old books. And besides Oualata is really not a city like our other cities, it has borrowed so much from everyone that it no longer knows what it is, too clever, certainly too coquettish for the rest of us prudish Bedouins, it has embraced the beauties of the Mali Empire when it was grand, it has taken everything from the Almoravids when they still had a faith, it has deceived the Moroccans, the Maqil Arabs, the fanatic Peul conquerors, the Oulad Mbarek, the Mechdhouf tribe, all of them thought they'd conquered it, but no, it deceived them all, it stole something from them, something essential, and then went back to what it still is, Oualata, coquettish but disdainful of what is not itself.

I tried to dissuade Sidi from going there. I used the children as a pretext: why haul them off on this punishing hike? Evelyn's father answered me: 'We want them to learn to confront the unknown, give them a taste of different things', the reflection of an intellectual rendered blasé by the comfort of large cities. Truthfully, I was wondering if I shouldn't stop, go to the nearest town and hold out my wrists to the dishonorable handcuffs.

While I wait, I doze off, gently rocked by the bumping of the car that's finding its way through the desert and the sand. Traveling these barren spaces now isn't even an adventure anymore, having a guide has become almost superfluous, there is the GPS, that devilish machine that shows you the roads, finished is the fear in your stomach, finished are the anxieties, the route is entirely laid out. If my father had one of these he wouldn't have gotten lost with the Cheikh, who wouldn't have been condemned to die, the GPS would have saved us all, me, my father, and my mother, too. And yet I can't bring myself to like this instrument that has stolen people's memory, the roads they've traced in their minds, the thousands of poems they've sung about the places and that help them to orient themselves now and then, yes, poetry served that purpose, too, of showing the way, I well remember the poem my mother taught me when I was very little:

> *Before you get to Lachgar*
> *You will first move up Leegal and its sharp rocks,*
> *The Titrin oasis, you'll see it in the distance,*
> *You'll keep going without turning around*
> *And you'll notice the Aranatt dunes*
> *Golden but hard to cross*
> *You will go east to go around them*
> *And the gorges of Amendel*
> *will open up before you*
> *Gaping wide to swallow up those who've strayed*
> *You will take the least arduous path*
> *On your right*
> *And if there is no wind*
> *You will see Mount Amendour in the distance,*
> *A small elevation and yet arrogant,*
> *Wearing the colors of the sky*
> *You will head there without turning around*
> *And right at your feet you will find a deep*
> *Well where you will quench your thirst*
> *Where you will give water to your mount*
> *Don't' spend too much time there for there will be*

*Only half a day more*
*Before you come, right in front of you,*
*To the Lachgar camps*
*The white smile of the Beloved*

This is how my mother remembered the places of her childhood. Yes, it's down there my grandmother once told me that they spent the winter months. And yet my mother has rubbed it all out, she even refused to join her husband when he fell in love with the great bare spaces. She buried everything, her past, and everything that connected her to my father.

But as I think about it, this poem is perhaps my father's. Ah yes, it must be by him, he sang it, and she's ashamed to mention his name, that much is certain. She wants to erase everything that has anything to do with him, everything, and in spite of it there are words that resist, there are times that refuse to fade.

I once caught a conversation she had with her sister. Aunt Verha didn't like me, I knew that, she never smiled at me, or brushed my cheek, she even tried not to look at me, I believe she wanted to banish me from her world, I bring back bad memories to her, she would dream of never seeing me again, but here I am, she's obliged to put up with my presence. So she was talking with my mother, and it went something like this:

'Why don't you tell him about his father? He must know...'

'Why should I? I'm afraid to hurt him, perhaps he won't understand.'

'But he'll find out one day, he's an intelligent boy, maybe he already knows.'

'As long as he knows it without my telling him anything.'

'But that's bad, really bad, he'll hold it against you, he'll hold it against us, all of us.'

'No, he's a sensitive boy with a generous heart.'

'You really think so?'

'I know my son.'

'That's what every mother says.'

'I am a mother.'

'That's not a reason, he has a right to know, it will make his life easier.'

'Don't you think that Ahmed and I are doing everything we can to make his life easy?'

'Of course, but he will know, and perhaps he will take it very badly and he'll ask questions about his father.'

'His father, his only father, is Ahmed my husband, and I am his mother, that's it.'

Why did Mama cling to that silence for so long? She was still submerged in it even when I already knew the whole story. She never truly spoke to me about my father, just a few allusions or some warnings concerning the bad character of my people. Now I know: she didn't want to awaken the volcano of love and hate that erupts when she mentions his name, for she had loved him very much, I surprised her as she was saying so, he abandoned her when she was pregnant and then he went off to follow new paths, true, but why did all of that have to fall on me?

In Oualata I like to sit for a moment on the meeting benches, where the city's sages would come together for endless discussions. I imagine voices being raised in the town's silence, for Oualata is a hushed city that lives very quietly but doesn't dream.

I'm far from everything. I am in a finished world, already dead. Oualata doesn't exist. Like Chinguetti, it only speaks in the past tense. How would the sleuths of our lazy police force find me here? They would need a time machine.

I'm rambling, sure, the cops only know the present. They won't get mixed up in grand theories. They'll search what's tangible, what's material, everything that's a clue, they'll circle around everything that's her. Her car for instance. It was parked in front of the Boutique Bleue. They will examine it thoroughly, they'll look everywhere, under the seats, in the glove compartment, under the chassis, they'll lift the hood, did anyone see her get in with me? Unlikely! And even if someone had seen us, they would have to know us for their testimony to be useful to the investigators. 'I saw her get into the car of some unknown person' wouldn't cut it. And why would that unknown be the assassin? How many people know both of us? I don't know. Isma certainly, and then a few of her girlfriends, that might make six or seven persons at the most, there are hundreds of thousands everywhere.

Ah yes, to find a clue they'll certainly search her car from top to bottom. But I was never in that car. Maybe they'll find plenty of fingerprints on her cell phone also, but nothing that can lead them to me, and so they'll be wasting a lot of time.

What's sure is that they won't find anything worthwhile in her car. She got out with the little red purse she was holding in her hand, I threw it out in the middle of the desert. They certainly won't find that. What was in it anyway? I didn't even go through it, probably some make-up. They'll analyze the contacts in her phone, had she listed my number there? I don't think so, she never called me.

A certain satisfaction runs through my body, I'm breathing fresh air, I feel overrun by a kind of happiness, it's as if I suddenly notice a small window opening freedom's door for me.

But what is this unnatural joy, what is this criminal thrill? I get up, suddenly gripped by my anxieties once again. I won't be able to live with this tornado inside me, it will swallow me whole every day, it will devour my entrails, it will light a fire deep inside me, no, I will suffer from it all my life.

No, tomorrow I will tell the whole story.

The narrow alleys are almost empty, a child running every so often, a woman who veils herself at my approach. Oualata has broken its ties with the world, I've always thought, it fell silent long ago, once every madness, every pleasure, all knowledge, every color, every ethnic group of the Sahara stopped meeting there, when the caravans died, when Timbuktu, little ungrateful sister, stole its men of letters, when caravan routes went around it, when the desert surrounded it with a belt of sand, when the muezzins' voice grew heavy. Then Oualata wrapped itself in a cloak of sorrow, primness, and pride, it decided to remain alone and kept its secrets from the ungrateful, it closed its doors to strangers and no longer offers them anything but the appearances of its lures, its sometimes fermented drinks, its exquisite dishes of squab, its mural paintings, the haughty smile of its virgins. It keeps the rest, the secret within its walls, to itself until the end of time.

So without any specific goal I wander around freely in a city that doesn't look at anything; then around the bend of an alley I notice a woman holding a kind of paintbrush, working on the decoration of a door. I stop to witness the birth. She doesn't turn around, she continues her meticulous work, absorbed in each little detail, I watch her hand, fascinated by the long, slender fingers that seem immobile and yet move, drawing lines, letters, mute and speaking forms on the sleeping wood. Then abruptly the woman turns around, looks at me for a brief moment, and goes back to her task. She must be in her fifties, she must have been very beautiful, she is still beautiful, her black eyes and long lashes, her graceful nose, her complexion must have struck more than one man. She gives me another look then goes back to her craft. Just as I'm about to leave, anxious not to disrupt her art any longer, she says in a calm, strong voice in which I hear a slight tremor, nevertheless:

'You must be Barhoum's son.'

At first I think I've heard it wrong.

'You look remarkably like Barhoum, you must be his son,' she repeats in a distant, falsely detached tone.

'Do you know him? Did you know him?'

She nods and goes back to her work.

Stunned, I stand there for a while, incapable of uttering a sound.

She seems to have forgotten me, too, she won't stop working, she doesn't turn around for a second.

I decide to wait for her, stay motionless while white shapes emerge from her fingers, I see them come alive, they aren't pictures, they aren't letters, but shapes going for a walk, scallops, straight lines, weird configurations that communicate nothing and everything, for a fascinating instant I feel my heart beating and waiting, I try not to cry out. She knows I'm there and she doesn't turn around, completely engrossed in her art. And then, while I thought her silence would never end:

'Your father, may God forgive him, was no saint.'

A shiver runs through my body, an acrid taste rises in my throat. I don't respond. Besides, she doesn't appear to be addressing me.

'And yet I know that he's innocent. The Cheikh's death, that cannot be his doing, no, he would have never done anything like that. It's true that he had no faith, he believed in nothing, he was just an egocentric hedonist, but that he wouldn't do, he'd never abandon anyone in the middle of the desert, he'd never steal anyone's water or money, especially not water, still he had no conscience, your father.'

I don't say a word. Her words don't offend me. I know that the people around here don't express themselves with such passion, they don't like to show their emotions. This woman, I say to myself, must have suffered a lot.

'How did you know him?'

'Ah, how did I know him? I knew him and that's all, knew

him a little too well, we used to see each other a lot, too often actually.'

'You were related.'

'And how!'

'What do you know about my father?'

'Everything, absolutely everything, but I've told you what's essential. He didn't kill the Cheikh, I will swear to that. And if you are his son you must know him well.'

'I never knew him.'

'True, you were undoubtedly not yet born when he died, or maybe you were just a baby.'

'What was he like, what did he think, was he a criminal?'

'I told you, I don't believe he was guilty of the Cheikh's murder. He must just have chosen, by himself, to face the desert with bare hands, he had that kind of pride!'

She picked up her brushes and I was afraid she'd leave without having told me everything.

'He was no saint? Why not?'

'He was a blatant liar, your father, a smooth talker, generous for sure, but disloyal like no other, a pagan who thought only about pleasing himself, and yet, he wasn't exactly ugly, and he knew how to laugh, he composed beautiful poems, only he was elusive, elusive... I wasted two years of my life waiting for him.'

'Were you engaged?'

'Yes, sort of, I don't know if I should talk about that.'

'Talk, please.'

'He promised he'd come back and I believed him. And then I found out that he'd gotten married, ah, how I despised him then. I think it was your mother he married.'

She quickly gathers up her brushes and leaves. For a moment I follow her but she doesn't turn around, I make a move to restrain her but my arm refuses to obey, I try to speak but the words refuse to come. She walks away, her step determined, she doesn't turn around, she refuses to look back, so I retrace my steps, she won't talk to me again, I know, she has turned the page, she goes off to find refuge from the memories of temptation. She's going to draw the strength from within herself to keep going, perhaps live with a surly husband, bawling children, wear the cloak of respect, a good woman of Oualata, pious and nondescript.

Out of the blue I see my father's ghost walking through the town, he was coming out of this house, walking these streets, loudly calling at the rare passers-by, he was dancing amid the stones, kissing the women, playing with the children, the surge of his laughter caused these placid walls to shake, these walls that were afraid of noise and would hide from emotions. As a man he was too present, I know that now, he took up all the space around him, his size, his likeable face, his large arms opening wide, his embracing look, all of it drew people's minds and hearts to him, he'd rouse the quiet spirits from their inertia, he'd pursue happiness, create it where there wasn't any, so misfortune had a grudge against him, set a trap for him, waited for him on a street corner.

Then all at once I feel exhausted, my legs won't carry me anymore, I sit down again in the shade of a wall, I'm tired of running in front of the dark silhouette of a father who flees from me, don't want to run out of breath following crazy images, shadowing shooting stars, and embracing horrors; why didn't you stick to reality, to the everyday truth, like everyone I know, they carry on without asking any questions, they only question themselves each day on the trivialities of that day, they don't run after delusions that are impossible to seize, they don't dream of always-renewed loves, they stay with their children and their wives, they go to the mosque on Friday where everybody sees them, they conceal their inner urges beneath fake smiles and hackneyed maxims, but they live, their children grow up, and sometimes they think they're happy; and you, what did you gain by running and trampling on the old wisdom of quiet minds, by burning the voice of ancient manuscripts, stomping on the false overwintering grass, shouting the truths that keep silent, tell me, what did you gain if not a name now reviled, the contempt of others, infamy, prison, this abandoned and suffering woman, and my mother's tears, what did you gain, tell me? And tomorrow you will be forgotten, your name won't appear anywhere anymore, finished, erased forever, I hate you, father, yes, I hate you.

I must free myself from this shadow that pursues me and never spawned anything but the wreckage of my mind, crushed my mother's youth, and left behind everywhere a deceptive smile and tears that do not evaporate beneath the burning sun, I am the last of its victims, quarreled with my family, rejected by my loves, I killed for him, yes, he really is the assassin who guided my hand, who clouded my mind, I must set myself free from it. Tomorrow I must denounce him and say that he guided my hand.

What would a judge's reaction be when I tell him that the real assassin is dead and that he used his son's hand to avenge himself and commit a crime?

Avenge whom? The Cheikh didn't actually indicate him as his assassin, he merely wrote that 'the guide abandoned us', that's not a real accusation, it could very simply mean that 'he left', which would then be no more than a simple statement, he surely couldn't manage any more words, he was dying of thirst, his dehydrated brain couldn't draw enough strength to say anything further. It was the others who blamed my father and killed him in the end, they turned him into a monster before putting him behind bars, a man like him couldn't survive inside the constriction and the lack of privacy of a prison cell.

And then I, why should I care, after all, whether my father is assassin or victim, he is who he is, dead, finished, and I am very much here, flesh, bones, a heart, a life, why was I so shook up when she said, 'I am the Cheikh's daughter after all', what was that trance that unsettled me so, that death gong that echoed in my ears, why did I become blind and mindless? I must be mad, that's it, I'm crazy and didn't know what I was doing.

But no, all my senses are intact, it was just one enormous cataclysm that came knocking on my door and I let it in, and now I've fallen into the crater of oblivion and cannot go back anymore, my old home looms in the distance but I don't even know how to reach it now, I have wiped away the traces that led to my past, I can't find myself anymore, tomorrow I must go to the city and say, 'it's me'.

But maybe if I had stayed, if I hadn't fled, this would have gone differently, nobody would suspect me. After all, do I really need to repeat it again, no one saw us together. So why not go back now? Call Mama first and tell her, 'I went with my friend Sidi to Adrar, I didn't have time to phone you...' And then go on living, perhaps with that agitated thing deep inside me that keeps on yelling. Living, I don't even know what that means anymore. Common everyday gestures, how would I even know how to salvage them?


My mother must be very worried now, she must be in a panic, a whole week without a sign from me, 'my little one...' is what she'd keep saying, she didn't see me grow up, 'my little one' is what she always called me, it sometimes upset me: 'I'm not a child anymore, Mama.' 'Of course, you are a man today, my little one.' But how could I not have thought of her before allowing the demon to explode? Why didn't I seek shelter in her arms to escape the bad djinns? Why didn't I think about her suffering and her tears for even one second? Now, it's finished, the muezzin of the end of the worlds has called. But I will always be ashamed to see my mother's tears flowing, suddenly I want to recite the poem by Mahmoud Darwish, '*I am nostalgic for my mother's bread, my mother's coffee, and I don't want to die because I feel ashamed to imagine the flowing of my mother's tears'*, or something close to that, but I don't have Moursil Khalifa's voice and I don't feel like singing.

And what about Ahmed, what will he think of me when he finds out? He won't believe it, that's for sure, he will refuse to believe it. In his eyes, I am a spoiled child, incapable of following anything through to the end, not even a felony, maybe he'll say it one time only and then he'll not mention it ever again, he'll file my case away somewhere and go back to his camels, of course he'll console my mother, he'll support her, he'll take every step needed to find me again, if possible even forgive me. But he will file my case somewhere inside his head, not that he doesn't love me, but he doesn't know how to be attached to things, he knows how to delete troubles, he possesses that aloofness that liberates and that balms the mind.

And what will Fati think? Perhaps she imagines that my act is nothing but despair over a lost love, that it's the result of the torment she caused me, 'I didn't know he loved me that much, loved me to the point of madness,' she'll say. She'll show some sorrow for me, but deep in her heart she'll feel the flash of a certain enjoyment. She knows how to turn everything back to herself.

Perhaps she's right, though? The sequence of things is so complex that I can't follow it. My father's disgraceful act definitely darkened our relationship. Maybe that played a role in my decline? No, that's absurd, long before I met Fati I was already haunted by the image of this father who was reviled by every tongue.

I went to see Amar, my father's lawyer, a man in his forties, with round eyes, silver-gray hair, known as the lawyer of lost causes, those that his colleagues refused to defend. He would take up the cause of wives who'd murdered their husbands, of blasphemers, prostitutes, homosexuals, it was his suggestion that he defend my father who immediately accepted.

'Ah yes,' he said to me, 'you are Barhoum's son, an interesting case, it wasn't easy, we had the crowd on our backs, they insulted me in the street, throughout the trial I was practically living underground, but I'm quite familiar with that rabble, you've got to let them bellow, hide from them a little, it'll pass soon enough and then you can raise your head again. But you know what, my boy, what I like in this profession is just that, look the bloody beast in the face, I almost won this trial my friend, yes, twenty years in prison is an absurd sentence that clearly shows the judges' awkward position, for if there hadn't been any doubt at all about his guilt he would have been condemned to death, especially since the entire audience demanded his head. So I proved the inanity of the accusation, but the judges couldn't acknowledge his innocence, that would have caused a riot and maybe the end of their careers, they would have been rejected by their colleagues and their loved ones, only twenty years and yet I swear to you, it didn't go unnoticed, the dumb ones grumbled, the Cheikh's followers raised their fists, just imagine what it would be if he'd been acquitted, the Taliban would have taken power', and he was laughing at this final witticism. I felt like grabbing him by the throat, dragging him into the street and shouting in front of everyone: 'Here's the guy who calls himself the lawyer of those without a lawyer, a profiteer in fact, who's found a way to gain recognition and who in fact believes in nothing!'

Would he defend me if I were arrested, maybe so, because the other lawyers would hang back, while he, he's afraid of nothing, maybe his family's name protects him, powerful people they say, but then, too, he demands huge fees. Who paid for my father? The people of his tribe obviously. Tightened their belts very firmly to be able to pay the ransom, yes, it really was a ransom.

In what way did this small-time lawyer actually serve my father? At the end of the day he was condemned to die, because prison was an ultimate sentence to him. He didn't die of dysentery, no, the prison food wouldn't have killed him if he still had a taste for living, but a man like him inevitably wastes away in prison, he lets himself die like certain caged animals, he doesn't know how to breathe the putrid air of incarceration, he's a man of wide open spaces, my father, a man of infinite horizons, of the interminable paths provided by the white sands and the rough terrain, how could he adjust to a cramped cell, occupied by small city thugs? I can imagine the distress, the despondency, that must have gnawed at him between four filthy voiceless walls, the rage at himself and at all of humanity that must have overwhelmed him, yes, I'm sure that he let himself die so he wouldn't have to witness his own deterioration, the pride that lived in him spoke and told him, 'you cannot live like an animal, you are a free man and nobody, no prison in the world, can rob you of that freedom'.

That's why I feel for him. But who says that it all happened that way, where has my imagination taken me, am I going to remain a prisoner of a myth that I may have created myself, is the idea I have of my father not embellished by my own desire to draw a picture of him that would boost my ego and justify my act?

But thinking about it carefully, did I kill for him? Wasn't it an irrational act? Why did I erase that resounding wallop Raya gave me from my memory until now? Yes, when she said, 'I am the Cheikh's daughter, after all', I think it's that 'after all' that enraged me, I answered: 'The false Cheikh? Ah, you're the daughter of that crook, but your father, what is he really if not a charlatan, and one of the worst at that?' That's when she whacked me hard, it might be that slap across the face that unleashed everything, madness took over and I jumped on her. Essentially I was only defending myself, at a trial I could well argue it was a legitimate defense.

I'm talking nonsense: killing for having your face slapped is not a legitimate defense and besides, I'm a lot stronger than she is, they couldn't present her death as the outcome of a fight, no, that's' absurd, I have killed, I am a criminal, and I shouldn't hide, everything has to come out, tomorrow I'll go and I'll say, 'it's me'.

But that blow certainly increased my anger tenfold, it was given a reason to be vented, if she hadn't hit me I might have just left her at the beach. She would've managed fine getting back to the city on her own.

But no, this is more nonsense, it came from my innermost depths, all my secret sorrows were awakened and threw themselves at her, my restless dreams, I was dreaming that's certain, I killed her in my dreams, but I killed her for sure.


Sidi set up our camp in the Oualata wadi, the rains haven't fallen in a long time and the residents have forgotten what course the water used to take. The reflections of the large lamp on faces and things give them an unreal blueish look, the city's shadows overlooking us accentuate the unreality, we're on another planet, I am Omom looking at the Earthlings pretending to exist, they bustle about in a watery fog amid colors and scents they can't imagine, they float on a sea of gray they cannot feel, they believe they're walking, they believe they're loving, they believe they're living, they're merely nightmare disturbances of a space monster that will soon wake up.

The specter of the large prison looms in the distance, initially it was a colonial army post that served to control the region, arrest the barbaric hordes of nomads that like wolves would occasionally launch an assault on the cities, driven by an idealistic madman, by the awakening of old myths or by hunger. Now it serves as a prison for political men and dangerous criminals, without a need for any prison guards, since all around Oualata there's desert, hundreds of kilometers of desert, fleeing means dying of thirst, for a big city dweller staying means dying of starvation and boredom because the food is too bland and the horizon is dreary, the prisoners would weaken before one's eyes and sometimes waste away.

Tonight I want to remain inside myself, I want to remove the world and the noises it contains, I feel a fire ball inside my throat and I cannot speak, I walk away from the camp and stretch out on the sand, hands under my head, the immense sky and the shadows of the old city, too, are watching me. I want to smother everything inside me, the madness that lies in wait and the questions that summon me, and even Mama's face and even Fati's mocking smile. Why am I the lamb they'll slaughter to ward off fate, why do suffering and doubt choose me as a refuge, what wouldn't I have given for a life without conflict, a path without deviations, the dull stillness of uneventful days. Tomorrow everything will stop because I will tell it all. I can already see the crowds roaring, the rage, the indignation, the invectives, the hate, my name and that of my father will forever join the long list of cursed men, but what does their hatred matter to me, I hate all of them as well.

Oualata is beginning to wound me, I have trouble with this city that reminds me of my father again, I read too much of our decline in it, 'our' I said, I've done nothing wrong and no original fault has the right to hound me, and what about him, did he really kill, is he really the monster the Cheikh's followers make him out to be?

It reminds me of a conversation I had with Fati, she attacked our societies, which condemned entire classes to stay locked inside sometimes dead-end occupations, I didn't feel concerned, I said that was all in the past but she countered saying 'no, it's still inside people's heads, it's a feeling of superiority that lives inside former masters even if they're poorer now', I didn't reply. I never find the right words with her, even if I'm right. But why should I remember her words? She's finished, Fati, as my existence is finished, as these now fading lights have already gone dead, first turning brown before they go down, tomorrow, through the redness of the sun, humanity will truly wake up and look at itself. Won't it be ashamed of what it has been?

Tonight I can't remember anything but the gurgling voice, the contorted face, the spittle coming from her mouth, the eyes as large as two full moons wanting to flee from the sky, did I squeeze harder to make the nauseating rumblings stop, efface the dreadful image? I finally let go of her neck and collapsed on the sand, she wasn't moving anymore, she wasn't speaking anymore, and what I saw was my father, he, too, was howling, loudly shouting to say he hadn't killed but that his son was the assassin, not he, I got up with difficulty not even glancing once at the body lying there sprawled beside me, I staggered all the way to my car to get away, run toward the unknown, toward the absolute silence where the cries from my stomach and the beating of my heart would maybe merge.

Néma, where I will tell the whole story, isn't far, and the tongues that will insult me won't matter, the dismay of my friends won't matter, and Fati's anguished smile and my mother's devastated face won't matter. In Néma I will tell it all and they'll put me in an old truck, handcuffed, to go back to the capital, and that old crate will stop in every little village and the curious will come and look in the back at the killer of the Cheikh's daughter, tied up, eyes fluttering, and they'll insult me and spit on my body...

Suddenly my anxieties and fears fell silent, breathless as I see the woman with the paint brush appear, gliding rather than walking on the sandy soil, the veil covering almost all of her face, but I recognized her easily, I'd already become familiar with her gait, I'd already defined her silhouette inside me, 'What is she coming for now? Talk to me about my father, the basics have been established, I know, I don't need to prod my pain nor have her relive hers'. With a bit of rage in me but shame as well, I moved toward her, hands held out and head down as if to humbly collect the bile she wanted to pour out, close my five fingers over her sorrow and carry it all inside me, me the legitimate heir to my sire's ultimate betrayals.

She stopped, and facing me, she looked me in the eyes

for a moment, as if to size me up again, weigh how much inhumanity my genes still held. I turned my head away but she followed me with her gaze, at that instant I wanted to die, vanish forever. Then she abruptly took a finely decorated box out from under her veil, opened it slightly with a swift gesture to show me some small objects: a henna-painted rosary, a stylized teapot, tea glasses embellished with minuscule colored dots, a tiny miniature of an Oualata mosque.

'This is for you,' she said simply, 'some small souvenirs from Oualata.'

I held out two tentative hands and could utter no more than a tremulous 'thank you', as she rapidly retreated.

I was tempted to call her but I couldn't, it all seemed so unreal and incredible to me. Why give a present to the son of the one who had tormented her, is it in memory of the happy moments they'd spent together or does she see me as another victim of my father's depravities, thereby sealing a type of solidarity between the two of us? I was holding the unusual gift in my hand and didn't know what to do with it.

Then suddenly my father's face appeared to me, smiling, his eyes alight with wonderful memories, his lips replete with a poem he wasn't reciting, the tail of his turban grazing the earth with a blissful but desperate kiss. Why then had I been ashamed of him for so long? He was an accomplished man, he loved life, he loved nature, he loved women, the sands and fine rain of clear mornings, the songs of dunes believed to be asleep, and the bellowing of camels nostalgic for long journeys, what harm is there in that?

Yes, but as an inheritance he gave me nothing, I didn't inherit his love of life, nor his appetite for existence, all these fine treasures evaporated with his final days, and he became nothing more than an assassin, a renegade, an enemy of God and men and he died asphyxiated by the narrow-mindedness he always refused, strangled by anger and misery, his memory is a burden for me today, yet I must learn to bear it.

But what good would a blood-stained diadem be to me, a diadem for me alone, loathed by everybody, can I, all by myself in this country, seriously fly my father's flag? It would be claiming the responsibility for both the Cheikh's and Raya's death.

The Cheikh is one thing, my father was innocent, I'm sure of that now, but I, how can I raise my head for even an instant while having the image in my eyes of that restless girl, strangled by a satyr on the beach.

The fire Mahmoud has lit is dancing in the middle of the night. It lights our faces with a pale elusive glow. The objects around us appear and disappear before the flickering light, the music of the crackling wood pampers the spirits. Above us Oualata seems to have lost consciousness, already sleeping a carefree sleep. As they wait for the meal my friends are dozing off, the day must have been exhausting for them, I'm a bit embarrassed that I let them go off without me. I should have accompanied them, it would have pleased them and, for a moment perhaps, I would have forgotten the demons eating away at me.

The children are quietly sitting in a circle showing each other lovely stones they've collected during the tour. Roger won't take his eyes off me. He's afraid I'll disappear. He whispers something in Natalie's ear who turns around and smiles at me. They've gotten the better of me, I know, I'll comply with their wishes, I'll look within to find a way to end the story. I don't know what to do with Omom anymore. Will he lead the Earthlings to recover themselves? Will he provoke a revolution to overturn the throne of the bad djinns? Will he recruit his own for a war to liberate the Earthlings, 'star wars' as Evelyne said, will he see the young Bedouin girl again and take her back with him to his distant planet, or will he break the neck of every bad Cheikh who impedes the earth?

Sidi stuffs us with food this evening. There is both Tajine and couscous and even a delightful dessert, dates from

Adrar. Fall scolds the children a little for eating too fast. The empire of tales calls me and I don't know how to respond, it's the single thread that links me to an appetite for living these past few days. I'm already dreaming of being a storyteller, just a storyteller, traveling the length and breadth of sands, forests, mountains, visiting oases, villages, cities, always surrounded by droves of children, always telling tales that make the eyes of the little ones shine. But tomorrow, in Néma, my wanderings will come to a close and so, this evening, I will have to end my story.

Besides, the children are already hanging around my neck demanding their dues. Roger has now baptized himself Omom, Evelyne is repeating the song I created for the young Bedouin girl. I won't keep them waiting.

'*So Omom started up his machine and rushed off again. He didn't linger over the cities he was looking down on, they went back to their true size, very tiny, very modest, he didn't converse with the chatty clouds who were laughing, nor with the stars who wanted to talk, or the meteorites that were walking around singing, he didn't glance once at the satellites the Earthlings had installed that were making disharmonious 'beep beep' sounds. His mission was finished, he knew it, it was pitiful, he knew that now, he only wanted to see the beautiful Bedouin girl once more before going back to his planet, which he should never have left.*

*Approaching the Sahara did him good, the sandy vastness he saw naked and mute, the camel driver he noticed, a small black dot in a golden universe stretching out without letting up, suggested a calm, deep truth.*

*Here, he told himself, people are just who they are, stripped of the trappings that civilizations produce, occupied solely with surviving, looking at the sky, and loving. The bad djinns wanted nothing to do with this area because they don't know how to blend in.*

*It was easy for Omom to find the white dune again where*

*he had landed before. The young girl wasn't there but he knew she
would come. He would wait for her. He lay down on his back and
watched the sky, night had fallen, a thousand stars in all their
finery were sparkling in frenzied competition. Omom knew them
well, he had caressed them, he had laughed at their airs, he knew
their beauty was stolen from the sun but that the generous king
of the stars had forgiven them, now they were dancing dressed up
in their loveliest clothes, but Omom was waiting for the lone little
light that had managed to move him. The machine he had with
him issued its first warnings, he paid no attention to it, he would
have plenty of time to activate it again and go back home.*

*The young Bedouin girl dropped down by his side as if
she'd come from heaven.*

*'I knew you'd come back,' she said with a small touching
laugh.*

*'Yes, I came back, my friend, to see you again.'*

*'Long ago, when I was still very small, my mother read in
the sand that one day I would meet a man who'd come from the
sky and who would love me.'*

*'Your mother is a good soothsayer.'*

*'No, my father says that when she predicts rain is coming,
you should expect a big wind.'*

*'He must have said that as a joke.'*

*'Yes, he jokes around because my mother knows every-
thing.'*

*'Does she know you have stolen the heart of someone who
was merely passing by?'*

*'All she knows is that an odd stranger may have bewitched
me and then left.'*

*'And that you stayed within him.'*

*''She didn't tell me that.'*

*'I went to a world that has lost its smile.'*

'Did you come across any greenery?'

'There's nothing but desiccation all over this big earth.'

'Yes, and because people have no joy in their hearts there's no delight in their eyes.'

'You say such truthful things.'

'That's because I know how to listen, my good friend.'

'It's also because here, where you live, one can hear the wind's lamentations and see the birth of the sky's first blushes, while everywhere else all across the world infernal noises occupy the ears and ghastly creations obstruct the horizon.'

'Have you seen the world?'

'I've been everywhere.'

'I would so much love to travel and see the world.'

'And would you come back?'

'Of course I'd come back.'

'You would come back without hands, without eyes, without a heart, because you will no longer know how to touch things, and things won't touch you anymore either, you'd only learn how to use them as if they had no soul, you'd wring the necks of the clouds, the wind, the rain, the dawning day, just to use them, too, and you won't know how to speak anymore.'

'You're frightening me.'

'No, I'm telling you what I saw.'

'When I was little, we used to know each time where we were supposed to go, the men would get up at the break of day and we'd take directions from the clouds, today the sky no longer tells its truth, my father likes to say.'

'Because they have depleted the sky, they've robbed it of everything. Tell me about your world.'

She got into a simple position, arms around her delicate legs, and softly began to talk about the life they were leading, the *slow progressions of their meager caravans, the never-ending daily toil, the exhaustion of the nights and then their elation when they'd break, when they'd find a bit of water to drink and some grass for their animals, and about the loves of the young girls, the certainties of the elderly, and the city-dwellers who would sometimes come to disrupt the serenity of time with their machines that pierced the earth and terrified the cattle, about places now prohibited from grazing, about farmers who frequently threatened them with their weapons, and then...*

*Omom felt his heart take wing. The moon had appeared without his being aware of it and was now watching him with its huge very white eyes, he touched his chest and found the object, but the machine had died and now only carried its supply of useless diamond. He looked at his distant star thinking he could cling to it, but the planet of the good djinns was glistening, impassive in the center of the firmament. The young Bedouin was still talking and he took her hand. She did not pull away. Then he fell into a deep sleep.'*

Mahmoud was already taking down the tents, the sun was sending a still timid glance to the earth, its first flames caressing the lazy clouds, the children ran around in the day's hot cauldron, while their parents were stretching to chase away the last of sleep's shadows. The morning light wrapped the city with a purple mantle, exquisitely coloring objects, all of nature seemed to be gradually waking up, the camels roaring loudly and shaking their ropes, knowing all too well what this brightness portends: the sky's fire will soon mate with the earth and will become an inferno.

But for me the inferno is inside and I no longer know where to go. I don't look at the sky or the sand at my feet. I'm wholly within myself. Now, I feel it, everything is sealed, the search must have found a way, Commissioner Dahoud is not a man to accept uncertainty, he must have swept away any ambiguities and set out toward a new horizon. He likes to indicate the guilty party rapidly or take a unique path for his arrest. Perhaps he has already pointed me out, perhaps he has definitively turned elsewhere, an innocent man or some elusive bandits or terrorists. I know with certainty that at this moment everything is closed, but I also know that from here on in my life will be nothing but wretched upheavals. Prisoner of the awful image of a dying Raya, of my eternal remorse, or locked up forever in a dark prison, slowly dying among the city's scum.

My friends are awake and seem much more cheerful. The children are still running around, thrilled with such expanse, their parents call out to them but they're bathing in the sea of sand and screaming loudly, they turn around me then wander off, I watch them, jealous of their innocence. Other children, their torsos bare, observe us from afar and don't dare come any closer. Sidi comes over to me.

'I know, you haven't slept.'

I don't answer, he annoys me immensely, since the beginning he hasn't stopped watching me.

'Tell me, if you have a problem maybe I can help.'

No, I won't tell you anything, Sidi, just as I won't tell anything to anyone anymore, I'm already in another sphere, I am a prisoner of other forces, I am elsewhere and I will not say anything, I've cut my ties with you, Sidi, and with the others, I died with Raya, sprawling lifeless on an almost deserted beach and perhaps I won't be resurrected until the day I pay my debt; no, neither my mother nor Ahmed will manage to save me because the filth is already in me, because the abject questions have already suffocated any voice in me, I am nothing but a brown slave who doesn't know where he's going, who can no longer flee the pain inside him because he now knows that the bondage is within him and that he will not escape from it, twenty, thirty years in the dungeon and I'll get out cleaner, memories less dense, aged, a gray complexion, lightless eyes, but the dreadful chains finally broken. Today, this very day, as soon as we arrive in Néma, I will tell all.

Néma has the face of days of fire, the sun seems to cover the homes and the eyes with its burning cloak, the inhabitants pass by quickly to escape from the sky's furor and find shelter, the occasional car rushes through the few avenues. I know, Néma isn't Néma anymore, the old city is dead and the new doleful, squalid quarters have trouble rising again; the old mountain, the only glory of which the poets sang, seems to have collapsed, nostalgic for ancient melodies too quickly lost. Néma certainly tried, but nothing works: the shadow of its past still hovers above it, a dissident city, born from the ire of notables who didn't acknowledge the new order        of the old oases and who only three centuries ago left their native Oualata to establish a new home. Néma has tried everything but has always wept over being only Néma, a prisoner of the celebrity of its two elders, Oualata and Timbuktu; it really wanted to mark its camp, Guelb Ndary, the mountain that overlooks it would be dressed in its finest attire in the rainy season, its old houses embellished their doors with arabesques designed by the finest artisans, but travelers would merely pass through and the griots would only drone on with their small guitars to boast about the suave beauties of other natures, although withered once and for all. No matter, tired of smiling Néma gave itself a severe grin that no longer winks at the insensitive travelers, its market swarms with incomprehensible noises and incongruous smells, its broad river of sand is flooded with bricks and debris, its new homes use placidity and ennui as make-up, the covering of its doors look worn, it no longer wants to wear any ornaments, it has no ambitions other than to remain itself. Its population, though, hasn't lost its original cheerfulness of happier days.

This time Sidi took his friends to a hotel, they'll have a long siesta and in some vague approximation will try to get back to today's conveniences: a shower with little pressure, a large bed that sags beneath the body, an air-conditioner that steadily moans and sometimes falls silent, electricity, the cell phone that finally actually crackles.

I know my father used to come through here often. I wait for everybody to be settled before I approach the maître d. He doesn't wear any livery, his wide boubou made of lightweight fabric floats around him, his face is marred by smallpox scars, he listens as soon as I come near him, surely used to discreet requests that will be quickly refused.

'I'm just curious to know. Did you ever meet a certain Barhoum, a state guide?'

He looks at me in surprise, then his face narrows with sudden certainty.

'You look a lot like him. Are you his son?'

'Yes.'

'He was my good friend. He used to bring his clients here. He was very funny, he loved life. May God forgive him!'

'Did he come to Néma often?'

'Oh yes, often, very often, it's true that he did no more than pass through, but half of the people in town knew him.'

'What did they think of him?'

'In the beginning they had a rather good opinion of him, despite, you know, his tribe...'

'Yes, I know.'

'Well, his name reminded people of too much plundering, but he was appreciated because he was always laughing and he would bring tourists but... '

'But?'

'Leaving a great Cheikh to die in the desert… well, I do understand him a little, in his place I would maybe do the same thing, I'd think about myself first, not to die of thirst, too bad for the others, no, I don't want to preach, but after al…'

'After all?'

'Well, the Cheikh had a very fine reputation here, as well as everywhere else.'

I don't continue the conversation, the verdict is obvious; he was found guilty here, too. He remains a pariah in people's minds, no attenuating circumstance has been granted him. For me as well they won't have anything but rejection, anger, hate, screaming jackals. I can already hear them shout, they live inside my ears, I will never be able to reduce them to silence, these howling masses who obstruct even the awareness I have of myself, who pursue me with their repulsive hatred. I won't wait any longer, I will go to them.

Sidi came to me again, observes me, you'd think he wants to have a word with me but nothing comes out, he just looks at me, slightly worried, makes a gesture but then stops, pretends to look away: the little moribund acacias you can see trembling in the burning zephyr of this fiery day. I head for the door and after a slight hesitation he follows me, one might say that he's afraid for me. I don't turn around, I don't want to turn around anymore, the furnace is in front of me, that's where I'm going now, I see Raya's twisted face again, the terror in her eyes, the spittle between her lips, then I see Fati, shaking her head, inconsolable for having loved me, and Mama, shaking with sorrow, and my friends, incredulous, thunderstruck. I swallow my tears, I repress the panic that lies in wait, no, I must stay strong, look life in the face, I must overcome what's tragic and to that end find a reason for it. Tomorrow will always be tomorrow. The days and nights are inscribed on the façade of time. Yes, I finally discover the missing word, the only one, which in its absurdity explains everything: fate. I'm destined to be torn from life, sent to dark dungeons, heir to a distant tragedy. I'm only a fragile tree that bends in the winds. All of it was simply a game, my questions, my anxieties, my enthusiasms, my joys, my loves, futile exercises of a destiny that laughs at me.

I just need to erase the images, no longer see what's awaiting me: rejection, suffering, and hate.

I suddenly hold out my hand to Sidi.

'Telephone!'

He gives me his cell phone without a word, as if struck by bewilderment. I dial Mama's number. It rings for a long time. I redial the number, one, two, three times, then a voice emerges from the void.

'Hello... hello...'

The sound seems far away, tired, breathing heavily, desperate.

For a few seconds I don't say anything, and that hello becomes a cry, a call for help.

'Hello, hello, hello.'

I can hardly speak, I simply say 'Mama' and then an enormous cry resounds on the other end of the world:

'Nadir, Nadir, Nadir, my little one.'

'I'm here, Mama.'

'I was afraid for you, afraid... '

'No, you shouldn't be afraid, Mama, I'm not afraid anymore. I know that what must be will be. Nothing really new can happen. Nothing that hasn't already happened.'

I sense Sidi fidgeting behind me, I hear him mutter. I move away a little.

My throat is hoarse. There's a quiver in my voice that I cannot suppress. Mama is stammering words, I hear nothing, crackling and then...

'Your mother suffered a lot from your absence, my son.'

'I went looking for oblivion. I wanted to close my eyes.'

'I know, you were sorry about your action.'

'More than my action, mother, I was sorry about my life. But now I understand that it's all laid out.'

'Yes, everything is written, my son, you must have faith, Ahmed and I... '

'I know you both love me, but it's certainly too late.'

'Don't say that, we're going to expunge everything, it will all be like before.'

'Like before? Impossible! My hands are soiled, Mama.'

'No, just a bad slip, that's all.'

'What are you saying, mother? A bad slip?'

'A temporary stupidity, rather, but everything will go back to normal...'

'Mama...'

'You don't risk anything anymore. Ahmed and I, we've seen the Cheikh's family. They don't want to hear anything more about the incident. Their reputation, you understand? And Raya herself...'

'Raya is dead, Mama...'

'Dead, what an idea, she left the hospital, more fear than pain, the emotion above all, Ahmed and I, we...'

The cell phone falls from my hand, a huge cry that reverberates in me becomes a dreadful shockwave surging through my body, everything slipping away, the sky, my legs, my ideas, I collapse. Suddenly, with no warning, I burst into tears.

## AUTHOR BIO

A francophone journalist and author of several novels and short stories, Mbarek Ould Beyrouk received the Ahamadou-Kourouma prize for his novel *Le Tambour des Larmes* (*The Drum of Tears*) and the Prix du roman métis des Lycéens. In 2023, his novel *Saara* was awarded the Prix Africain.

## TRANSLATOR BIO

Marjolijn de Jager is an award-winning translator and scholar of francophone and African literature. She is the English-language translator of Beyrouk's novel *Pariahs*, published in 2023 by Schaffner Press, as well as works by Yasmine Ghata, Emmanuel Dongala, Louis-Philippe Dalembert, and she is a recipient of the Villa Albertine Award for excellence in translation.